Gatwick Bear

and the Secret Plans

Anna Cuffaro

Illustrations by Anna Anguissola

Sparkling Books

A CIP catalogue record for this title is available from the British Library.

1.0

BIC code: YFC

ISBN: **978-1-907230-02-8**

Printed in Great Britain by the MPG Books Group, Bodmin and King's Lynn

Visit our website *www.sparklingbooks.com* for further information.

Chapters

1 Homeless

It was early one Thursday morning when security first spotted a bear cub roaming around London Gatwick Airport over their CCTV system. They couldn't believe their eyes. But, there he was, in the departures area, as large as life trundling around a big box on wheels, tied up with red rope, and a small blue Edwardian case with rusty catches and an even rustier big lock. He was wearing a navy blue waistcoat done up with a row of shining golden buttons. Security couldn't make out whether the bear was coming or going. Did he just land and get lost? Was he about to catch a plane? They didn't know that the bear had actually lived at Gatwick Airport for some time and that he wasn't a passenger. Oh, no! He was homeless. And, all he had in the world was in that luggage.

Security decided not to catch him straightaway. They pointed their camera on the bear and spied on him to see what he was up to. They saw him park his luggage and then he rode on baggage trolleys jumping from one to the other while they were moving. He had this idea that if he kept moving around he wouldn't get caught, and he knew full well that you're not supposed to live at an airport. But he had nowhere else to go. Anyway, he soon got fed up with riding around, so he started window shopping at the airport stores. The bear had never bought anything, of course, he had no money. At the coffee shop, he usually found some leftover coffee, cold but drinkable, and scraps of chocolate muffins. Sometimes he found muffins on or under seats or in the bins, but today he had to crawl under a table to get one. He so adored chocolate muffins.

Next the bear made his way to the pizza hut. There were always scraps there, too. Then, like he always did after breakfast, he went to the men's toilets, gave himself a quick wash all over, brushed his fur nicely but only down the front, he couldn't reach round the back. He was very proud of his fur, though it was often a bit ruffled because it just wouldn't stay down.

Gatwick Airport was the best place in the world. It was clean, warm, safe and shiny. But his favourite place, his very favourite place in the whole airport was the broom cupboard. Every night, when the last planes left and night fell over the airport, the bear slept there snuggling up to the biggest mop, who he thought must have been some distant relative of his. He would run and hide under the mops when he saw a police officer or anyone else in uniform.

At night when he couldn't sleep, sometimes the bear would have fun sorting out the cupboard for the cleaners. He loved the coloured liquids. All the reds on the top shelf, all the yellows in the middle, and all the greens at the bottom – just like traffic lights. The cleaners knew all about the bear cub. They had often seen him in the cupboard. But the cleaners didn't tell security. The cleaners called him Gatwick. He became their mascot and they were very fond of him. To repay the cleaners for their kindness, Gatwick kept the cupboard tidy; he rearranged the mops for them when they threw them in the cupboard after use. Gatwick would place all the yellow mops in the left-hand corner, all the blue ones in the right-hand corner, all the brooms at the back against the wall, and the buckets in a high stack in the middle, and he'd fold up the dusters.

The cleaners should have told on him but, if they had done that, Gatwick would have been turned out onto the streets. Sleeping in the cupboard also meant he wouldn't be shone on by those big neon lights fixed to the ceiling all over the airport. Such horrid things, they were on all night and used to stop him sleeping before his cupboard days. Gatwick himself didn't know how long he'd lived at the airport. In fact, he didn't know if he'd been born there, if he'd been lost there, or even if he'd been found. He didn't know much about himself at all really, except that he knew for sure that he had no family. He also knew that he was not like anyone else he'd seen at the airport. No, he was certainly different. Much more hairy for a start.

Every night before he switched the light off in his cupboard, he took out his map of the airport. When he found a piece of muffin, he would draw a muffin in the spot where he had found it. That night he drew a muffin under the table at the coffee shop. Gatwick had a feeling that there were lucky places in the airport, and he wanted to remember where they were. He had already drawn five muffins on the map.

Security were now ready to deal with him. The dreaded Miss Acid, Head of Security, set out on his trail. Her nails were pointed and varnished black with silver tips – more like claws, really, which were as sharp as her eyes. Her hair was worn in a painfully tight bun which stood up straight on her head. It was so tight that it drew all the skin on her face upwards and distorted her ugly face. She terrified everyone at the airport. She wore flat shoes and was thick around the hips. She had to keep discipline in the airport – maximum discipline. Let me tell you if you don't behave, she'll throw you straight into a prison cell. Just don't argue or be cheeky

5

to her. There were rumours going round that she threw furry creatures in the cement mixer on the building site next door: cats, dogs and mice who wouldn't stay away from Gatwick Airport. Miss Acid only liked feathered creatures: especially eagles, vultures, hawks and ravens. One day, she caught a gigantic raven using her bare hands and a strong brown net used by hunters: "Let me out! Let me out!", the raven squawked. But Miss Acid whisked him up and shut him up in her locker. There he would stay until she had time to buy a cage. He was now her pet and she named him Jet. Gatwick knew this because he had seen it all with the eyes in his head and heard it all with his furry ears.

Well that was it. Gatwick was cornered too. Miss Acid looked at him with dreadful suspicion: "Hey, little fellow, and where do you think you're going?", she asked with her voice rising dangerously to an incredible squeaking pitch. Gatwick stood there with his serious round face and watery eyes. His ears stood to attention as he stammered out in his little voice:

"I... I... don't know exactly... where..." Without giving him time to finish she shrilled:

"Get out of the airport this second. You are nothing but a detestable furry creature".

"What did she mean by that?" thought Gatwick.

Whatever it was, she didn't sound pleased to see him. She

didn't like his fur. 'Maybe I should brush it all in the other direction', Gatwick thought looking down at his ruffled paws. No matter how much he brushed his fur down, it did insist on sticking upwards, on end. So Gatwick began to feel ... quite odd.

"Maybe I don't belong here. In future, I will just have to keep moving around even more to avoid being caught. I will have to hide behind newspapers or under the seats in departures", Gatwick thought.

Anyway, she marched him to the door and, as she threw him out in the dark and the rain she shouted: "And, don't come back again!" But this was his home! That night he slept on a hard wooden bench in the scary pitch black and hollow bus shelter. The rain bucketed down sideways, and all his fur got soaking wet.

2 Departures

Always the happy chappy, Gatwick would not let Miss Acid get him down. The next morning, he sneaked back into the airport wearing a pair of sunglasses and fake sideburns. Everything Gatwick had, he'd found in or around the airport. And he crammed all these items in his luggage.

He'd never been abroad before though he'd lived in departures all his life. The time had come to get away from Miss Acid and fly away somewhere. Gatwick looked up at the departures board. "Hmm!", he thought. "I'd quite like to go to the mountains".

"Let's see", he scratched his head, "yes, Switzerland. They have big mountains there called the Alps. I want to climb to the top of one of those".

In the brochures scattered around the airport Gatwick had seen the Alps – they looked as if they'd had icing sugar sprinkled over them through a mega-gigantic sieve. They looked so good to him because he had such a sweet tooth. After all, he was just a cub. And, the chocolate they made in Switzerland also looked so scrumptious. He would like to try some of that.

The flight to Lugano City, Switzerland was open for check-in. 'Sector B', indicated the board:

"Oh, dear! Where's that?"

He looked all around him until a big letter 'B' caught his eye.

"That must be it", Gatwick thought, putting his finger on his chin. He did that when he was thinking.

"Can I check in for this flight, please?", he asked politely.

"Do you have a ticket?", the young woman at the desk asked.

"Yes, of course". Gatwick gave her the travelcard he'd found in one of the bright shiny bins. He loved those bins, a treasure chest of things he needed.

"Well, I'm afraid this ticket is not valid for travel on our airline".

"Could you tell me which airline accepts travelcards, please?"

"No airline will accept your travelcard, I'm sorry", she answered back.

In his everso polite voice, Gatwick pointed out that she had said that her airline wouldn't accept his travelcard, so it meant that some other airline would accept it.

So Gatwick went off, wandered round and round some more, until he found a young woman in a different colour uniform. She looked very friendly. She might let him on her plane. No, she wasn't friendly at all. She wouldn't let him on her plane either. When, lo and behold, Gatwick saw another furry creature! It was dangling from the hands of a little girl. Her family was walking towards Passport Control. He followed them, maybe if he got to Passport Control they would give him a ticket. There was a notice saying he had to get his passport ready at the page showing his photo. Gatwick did have a passport – well, it was a photocopy of one, really. He had found a real passport one day, so he photocopied every page, cut around the edges carefully, coloured the cover in dark red crayon, then he pressed his face on the glass of the photocopy machine and reproduced his head. It was a big photocopy and didn't fit in the passport, so he carried that separately.

The official checked the family's passports and then asked if Gatwick was with them.

"Yes!", cried the young girl.

"OK, you can go through", said the official. Without looking at Gatwick's picture, the official ushered Gatwick through without giving him a chance to ask for a ticket. The little girl wanted to keep Gatwick; her father firmly said: "No". She had enough bears to look after as it was. Anyway, Gatwick didn't want to belong to anyone. Being stuck on a book shelf gathering dust was not his idea of fun. He wasn't a member and the president of the Freedom for Bears Club for nothing.

Gatwick felt so sorry for the bear hanging from the girl's hand. She was a cub, too. A very sweet-looking bear: all white with red ears, a cherry-red, heart-shaped nose, red soles on her paws, and a red dickie-bow round her neck. She was so beautiful! He was sure she was his little sister.

Gatwick found himself in front of a tall metal archway with red and green lights flashing every now and then. He thought that was splendid – a game of some sort. People were taking their shoes off, and their belts, and their jackets while drinking water and then aiming their bottles into big bins. As usual, Gatwick was only wearing his navy blue waistcoat. At Christmas, he also wore a red neck-tie. But it wasn't Christmas now. Gatwick went through the archway. Red lights started flashing fast and a loud buzzer sounded. Sheer joy! He must have won a prize.

"Could you remove your waistcoat please, sir? I think your brass buttons are setting the alarm off". So it was his buttons that won him the prize! They were beautiful buttons, no doubt. The buttons had FBC, for Freedom for Bears Club, engraved on them. But Gatwick couldn't take his waistcoat off because it was sewn on him. The officer tugged and tugged until he finally realised it was no use carrying on. So he gave up and let Gatwick through.

Now Gatwick was faced with another man: "Let's open your case, please, sir". Gatwick opened his suitcase. The Customs man took out Gatwick's green, yellow and red fishing rod, his wooden spoon and his other waistcoat. His spare waistcoat was red. Spare didn't mean that he wore it when he washed his other waistcoat because he never washed it. Oh, no; it meant that he would wear the red one, if he ever ruined the blue one.

"Did you pack the case yourself, sir?".

"Yes, I did".

"Has anyone tampered with your luggage?"

"No, they haven't".

"Are you travelling on business?"

"No, I want to climb mountains and fish in sparkling blue lakes", he answered happily.

"Excuse me, sir, do you mind my asking you a personal question?"

"No, of course not. Fire away".

"Why are you taking a wooden spoon with you?"

"For stirring and for all sorts of emergencies", Gatwick explained. The customs officer scratched his head and let Gatwick through.

What a cool place this was! Even on this side, there were shops. People were sitting around in armchairs drinking coffee out of small cardboard buckets. Gatwick was thirsty. Mmmm. No, he didn't want coffee. A fizzy drink would be better. He saw a queue and joined it. When it was his turn, he couldn't make up his mind what colour fizzy drink he wanted. The girl behind the counter started to roll her eyes up with impatience.

"Could I have an orange fizzy drink, please?" he asked. "But I haven't got any money".

"Look, if you haven't got any money, you're just wasting my time", she answered.

She gave him a small cardboard bucket of ice and ordered him to get out of the way so she could serve the next customer. Gatwick held the bucket in his furry paws, until the ice melted, and it was ready to drink.

3 Arnold

Gatwick went to sit next to a Polar Bear in a pin-striped suit. He was going to the North Pole on business. His name was Arnold. Arnold told Gatwick that he was big cheese in import and export. Gatwick asked him what that meant. "It means", Arnold began, "that you get things from one place and take them to another. I'm a frontrunner in that, you see?" Gatwick blinked. Arnold got slabs of ice from the North Pole and sold them to businesses all over the world; priced at affordable two shillings for big slabs, one shilling for medium slabs, sixpence for small slabs, and a thrupenny bit for a cube. Arnold was rich and generous:

"Hey, take this", Arnold said as he tossed a coin in Gatwick's direction, "let me give you a silver shilling, have a drink on me!".

His city-based company was called North Pole Iced Solutions and sold thousands of slabs. Ice had many applications especially in the building sector: ice bricks got rid of noise pollution and, if ice was placed in a bucket in the middle of a room, it could be used as environmentally friendly air-conditioning.

Arnold's mobile phone rang, he looked at the number and answered: "Hello, Anton Weiss speaking. ... Yes, I sent them to you yesterday ... it'll take a few days ... I'll do my best...

Goodbye". Gatwick wondered why Arnold had said his name was Anton Weiss on the phone.

Arnold apologised for the interruption. He was a great electronics fan. He even had an e-pen. There was a transmitter in it. It picked up waves and turned them into strokes on his computer. The pen was linked to his mobile phone and this meant he could transfer all his phone calls into written words on his computer as he spoke. Then he could instantly message these calls to all his colleagues. He was planning on getting optical character recognition so he could transfer pictures too. Gatwick got so bored that he had fallen asleep. Arnold shook him and started telling him how his business might come to an end: "But, the ice-cap is melting now; the sea level will rise, the ice won't be able to hold back the glaciers, which will flow into the ocean six times faster than now. Small islands will disappear under water. The Larsen ice-shelf has broken off, the Wilkins ice-shelf fell off, and I sold the other ice-shelf to the English bit by bit. The world is getting warmer and warmer. It's getting so hot that trees and other plants have been growing further up mountainsides to get away from the heat. Some types of plants are now extinct. The ecosystem is really messed up. There are deadly storms and floods, there are incredible forest fires and fatal heat-waves. And when the ocean heats up, a nasty acid builds up and kills sea life. Fish will be left gasping. The Amazon forest will turn into a desert. Tropical insects will breed and breed, and get bigger and bigger. Apart from that, it's not as dramatic as the Climate Change people make out".

Gatwick had fallen asleep again, but Arnold went on talking.

"We've had to cancel our training programme at the North Pole Iced Solutions Training Centre. All my employees will have to be laid off. And you know what that means? It means that the stress in families will lead to violence amongst cubs..." Arnold was interrupted by an airport announcement: "This is the final call for Mr. Arnold White booked on Flight NPA590 to the North Pole. Mr. Arnold White please proceed to Gate 3 immediately. The captain will order closure of aircraft doors in five minutes".

4 The Refuse Collector

Now Gatwick had to look for his own departure gate. He looked around him, when, all of a sudden, he saw Miss Acid telling some Italians off for playing football at the gates. She took their ball and cut it in half, there and then. On tip-toe Gatwick headed for the nearest pillar. Standing straight up against it, he took a deep, deep breath and pulled his tummy in. He peeped round the pillar to see her checking people's boarding-cards and passports.

"You were much younger then, weren't you dear?", she barked to a middle-aged woman thrusting her passport back at her.

Quickly, he pulled his head back. Oh me, oh my, she was coming his way. Gatwick jumped into the waste bin nearby. Miss Acid couldn't walk and think at the same time. She wandered around aimlessly for a bit then stopped to think about where to go next. By the time she had worked out that she wanted to look in the waste bin, a refuse collector stepped out in front of her, took out the plastic bag (with Gatwick in it), tied it up in an extra-tight knot, and hurled it into his wheelie bin. Gatwick knew how waste management worked at the airport. He had to escape from that bag before they sorted all the bits of him out for recycling. The sound of the refuse lorry moved closer and closer to his furry ears. The bag containing Gatwick was thrown on a heap. After a few moments, something started tapping on his head. The top of the bag was torn open by the yellow beak of Jet the raven. He was looking for food after a lucky escape. "What are you doing inside a rubbish bag?", Jet asked.

"I was trying to get away from Miss Acid. And, how did you escape?"

"Well, that's a long story", Jet answered. "Miss Acid and other officers were having a party. They'd had a bit to drink and started throwing bottles and cans around. Miss Acid had pushed those who were most drunk to the back of the room. Then a lad started aiming bottles at my cage from a distance. The cage toppled over. When the lad saw the cage on its side, he ran over, lifted it up and tossed it in the air. In a twist of fate, the door opened and I managed to get through it and fly away".

"How lucky !" Gatwick exclaimed. "But I must rush off now because I'm flying to Switzerland".

"Really? I've always wanted to go there, too. I'll race you. See you in Switzerland at Lugano City Airport!" Jet pecked a kiss on Gatwick's chubby cheek. While walking away from Jet, Gatwick turned around and beamed a big smile at Jet: "The first one there waits for the other one. Bye!"

5 Gatwick's Luggage

Now Gatwick had to go and look for his luggage. He had to figure out where he had seen it last. He had forgotten, of course. Maybe he ought to go to lost property. He went to the information desk. "Please, Miss", he began, "do you know where I can find my lost cases: a big box on wheels, tied up with red rope, and a small blue Edwardian case with rusty catches and an even rustier big lock? I left them around here about half an hour ago".

"I'm sorry, sir, but all abandoned luggage is taken to our North Terminal and placed on the mountain of lost cases in a field nearby". She looked into the monitor of her computer and continued: "There are, just a moment please while I answer the phone ... Sorry, as I was saying, there are 42 thousand pieces there now. Are you insured?"

"What's that?", Gatwick asked.

"Well, never mind. I tell you what. Why don't you go to North Terminal and look for your luggage? Your flight is late, you have time. We operate a free bus service between here and North Terminal. It stops right outside here". She gave Gatwick a note to show to the security guard who would let him back in.

So Gatwick went out and waited for the bus. He couldn't see the bus coming. As he often did to pass the time of day, he started whistling his favourite tune, *Knees Up Mother Brown,* while moving his round head from side to side and tapping one of his paws to the tune. He had nearly finished whistling the tune, the third time over, when he saw the blue airport bus approaching. He clambered up the steps and sat in the front row near the window. He'd have the best view from there. The wheels of the bus started going round and round, and off he went.

The bus eventually drew in to North Terminal. Gatwick ran, as fast as his paws would take him, to the field. There was a mountain of cases – of all colours and sizes – how could he find his big box on wheels, tied up with red rope, and a small blue Edwardian case with rusty catches and an even rustier big lock? But, he was a very determined bear. He clambered over hard-shelled suitcases, feather light suitcases, expandable suitcases, backpacks, sports bags, and even a trunk. He climbed back down a little and went up towards the other side. Ah, he spotted his big box on wheels, tied up with red rope and his small blue Edwardian case with rusty catches and an even rustier big lock. Holding on to his luggage as tight as he could, he ran and ran back to the bus stop. When our bear arrived at South Terminal, he was just in time to catch his flight.

6 Gatwick Takes Off!

Gatwick placed his big box on wheels, tied up with red rope, in the overhead locker and his small blue Edwardian case, with rusty catches and an even rustier big lock, under the seat in front of him. His happiness was complete when he settled down into his window seat. But he couldn't see out of the window; he was too small. So he stood on his seat and fastened the safety belt around his knees. What excitement! The flight attendant ordered Gatwick to sit down. "But I can't, I'm looking out for my friend, Jet. I'm racing him to Switzerland. I want to see when we overtake him".

"You must remain seated for take off", she ordered, "but you can stand up when the green light goes off. What does your friend look like? I can ask the pilot to tell me if he flies past, over or under your friend".

"Oh, would you really? Thank you very much! You'll soon recognise him: he's got ever such black feathers and a yellow beak. And he's my best friend. He saved me from getting minced up in little bits".

Gatwick carefully kept his eyes glued to the light above his head. When the seatbelt sign finally went off, Gatwick unfastened his safety belt and started jumping up and down on his seat with sheer excitement. He loved playing race-the-raven. Gatwick pressed his furry nose against the window and kept a lookout for Jet.

7 Jet's Adventures

By this time, Jet was flying over Paris. He was swooping down, down, down, because he wanted to perch on the top of the Eiffel Tower for a rest and a bite to eat. There was a restaurant on the second level where Jet found left-overs of snails in garlic butter. While Jet was sitting on the pinnacle of the Eiffel Tower, admiring the view from 1,063 feet high, he suddenly heard piercing police sirens: 'What's all that about?', thought Jet. The French had intercepted an alien object on the top of the Tower. Not only the police, but all the French authorities were in alert. And, the secret service had informed the President of France:

"We must take immediate action", the President ordered, "our security alert level must move up to scarlet. Do you hear?"

When the police, fire brigade, ambulances and onion vendors arrived, Jet thought it time to fly off. He soared up, up, up, until he was cruising at 15,000 feet, the same as Gatwick's plane. Soon Jet had to fly higher still because he was coming up to the Alps. What a beautiful sight! All those icing-topped peaks. The highest of all the mountains, in the Alps, is Mont Blanc – the White Alp – it is about 15,780 feet high. It's so high that if they are not careful planes and ravens can crash into it. But Jet wasn't flying over that particular mountain today, nor was Gatwick. They were flying over other mountains, and Jet could already see them in the distance.

So Jet was flying quite happily minding his own business, when two gigantic birds started circling around him. "Stop!", one of them squawked at him. Jet didn't stop because they looked like thugs.

"You are trespassing; this air space is ours".

"I can fly anywhere I like", answered Jet, challenging them.

One of the birds signalled to the other and shouted: "Go and get him, buddy".

Jet flapped his wings as fast as they would go: harder and harder, harder and harder, but he couldn't get away from these bullies, they were stronger, bigger, and it was two against one. They bullied all birds who flew over the Alps because they said it was their space. Everywhere they liked was their space, even if it wasn't theirs at all. If they wanted a place, they invaded it. They bullied the native birds to: "Get the hell outta here". The Eagles were all over the world, not just here. There were lots of them in England, too. They created land, sea and air bases wherever their whim took them. These particular Eagles were big-time bullies: they were from the Assault Battalion of the Air Cavalry, and the Alps were their area of operations.

They would beat you up first and then ask questions. Jet didn't know all this because he had only flown low over Gatwick Airport until this adventure began. What a sheltered life he'd had!

One of the Eagles grabbed Jet by the scruff of the neck, while the other started pecking him hard in the chest: "We'll show ya who's got the power and the glory around here, buddy! When we say stop, ya stop, ya jerk". Jet couldn't understand what he meant, but he it didn't sound good.

"Hey, Sam that's enough for now", Bird Dog squawked, "ya'll kill the thing. We wanna talk to him first. Let's take him to base camp".

Their headquarters were on Mont Blanc; the Eagles called it White Alp. That's where the commander sat. He was the boss, judge and jury: his name was Stud. Bird Dog was important, too: he was the air controller. Whether birds or planes, he decided who could fly over his head and who couldn't. Sometimes they shot birds dead either for fun or to practise their skills. If planes they didn't like, didn't stop, they would shoot those down, too.

Stud and Bird Dog operated from a bunker dug into the hard rock of White Alp. The bunker contained secret communications equipment. They also had a fleet of spy aircraft which were turbo-charged Eagles equipped with rockets, mini-guns and telescopes. Most of these Eagles wore medals for their valour.

The Eagles were digging into Jet again quite badly. It was at that very moment that Gatwick's plane overtook Jet. Gatwick had seen the treatment his friend was getting – Gatwick became very distressed and started crying. He pressed the button above his seat and called the flight attendant. "My friend is being bullied by Eagles, please stop the plane", he cried.

"I don't think we can stop the plane, but I'll go and talk to the pilot and see what we can do".

She soon came back with a big box of tissues. "I'm so sorry the pilot can't land here. Please accept this with our compliments". She gave Gatwick a box packed with goodies.

Two triangular shaped tuna sandwiches, a chocolate bar, a fizzy drink, some paper, and five brightly-coloured crayons. Gatwick started eating and drawing, it helped keep his mind off Jet. When he had finished drawing the inside of the plane, he drew a picture of a bear cub where his little sister was sitting. Then he pressed the button again.

"Would you like to see my drawing?" he asked the attendant.

"You are such a clever bear", she smiled. "I will give you a scratch card for your drawing. Prizes go from £1 to £20,000".

Gatwick didn't know what a scratch card was, but it looked fun. He pulled out his small blue Edwardian case, with rusty catches and an even rustier big lock, from under the seat in front of him and took out his wooden spoon. It was ideal for scratching; he sometimes scratched his back with it, those bits he couldn't reach with his paw. He scratched the card brilliantly, scratched it all off – he'd always been very neat. Then, he started reading: 'Con...grat...u... la... tions!' It took Gatwick a minute or two to get through the word – it was very long as far as words go. Then he continued: "You have won £20,000". These words he read quite easily, but the number foxed him. He could only count up to ten. Again, the flight attendant was called. It was the first time someone had won the top prize since she'd been with the airline:

"Oh, my God, I don't believe it!!" she screamed at the top of her voice.

Everyone on the plane wondered what had happened, a couple of elderly ladies at the back of the plane started panicking, had put on their life jackets, and were making a terrible noise, trying out the whistles, while heading for the emergency exit behind them ready for evacuation.

"No, it's all right, sit down, please. Gatwick's won top prize! Twenty-thousand pounds!"

All the passengers and crew started clapping and cheering. Gatwick even got some pats on his furry back. And the other bear cub on board, his little sister, kissed him on his cheek. He liked all this attention, because he was a bit of a show-off at heart. Some people were taking pictures of him waving the winning card in one paw and his wooden spoon in the other. Then, everyone started calling out for scratch cards. The attendant ran for her purse and bought ten for herself first, then she started selling scratch cards to the front rows, while another hostess started in the middle and the other from the back. Soon everyone on the plane was scratching cards, even the pilot! The lady next to Gatwick asked if she could borrow his wooden spoon. She was certain it was a lucky wooden spoon. But, it was no good. Nobody else won anything. After all this excitement, the passengers calmed down and prepared for landing.

Gatwick hadn't forgotten his friend. As soon as he landed, he would go to the police and tell them about Jet. But, first, he wanted to free his little sister.

8 The Eagles Question Jet

Jet was taken to a high security bunker built in concrete and steel. Over the entrance, lights changed from red to green as he was pushed in through the anti-atomic door. Then Jet was shoved into an elevator going up floor by floor until he reached the seventeenth level. The doors slid open to reveal the biggest and most threatening Eagle imaginable sitting behind a heavy wooden desk. There were two big phones on the desk, a black one and a red one. This was the Chief: Stud.

"Hiya, Buddy", Stud began. "Listen, I ain't here to frighten ya. All I want is a bit of co-operation. Let me tell ya before we start: it pays to tell the truth. My friends here", he shouted, pointing to his body-guards standing behind Jet, "ain't got good manners. Y'know, their moms brought 'em up rough, real rough. Know what I mean, Buddy? They just ain't got no manners".

Jet simply nodded because he couldn't find his voice.

"Now we're gonna record this conversation, so ya better be careful what ya say. Are ya in a secret service of any type?"

A secret service! Jet didn't really know what he meant. He thought hard. Well, he had escaped from Miss Acid and secretly came to Switzerland. Only Gatwick knew about that apart from himself.

"Well, yes, you could say I am".

"Who're ya working for? Who sent you to fly over that area of the Alps? Threats come to us from many sides".

Jet didn't know how to answer that. The bodyguards started closing in on Jet.

"Look Buddy", Stud continued, "I ain't here to pass the time of day. Let's get down to business. We got Red-tailed Hawk next door, he just loves torturin' prisoners in those prison cells out there. You ever seen one of 'em hawk birds? They gotta wing-span of four feet, wouldya believe it?" Stud signalled to one of the bodyguards who got hold of Jet's tail and twisted it hard.

33

Jet squawked out loud. "Well, together with Gatwick we decided to..."

"Now this Gatwick guy. Don't ya go thinkin' we dunno him. We've been keepin' an eye on him. He's dangerous. Where's he from? Do y'know where he was born?

"He just appeared. I think he was born at Gatwick Airport, or he was lost or found there. Nobody knows".

"Nobody knows, eh! Nobody knows, eh! Who are you working for?"

"I don't know".

"So how come ya guys are in secret service and ya don't who ya working for? Whose side are ya on?"

"All sides, I suppose", Jet thought that might be the best answer. Better to keep it general, if you didn't know the right answer.

"Look, Buddy, let's stop messin' around here. I'll tell ya what we're gonna do. Me and you are gonna be good friends. Y'know, us feathered creatures have to stick together. Birds of a feather...! and all that baloney you come up with in London, like proverbs and rhyming slang". Then Stud started talking to his bodyguards: "Hey, guys, whatya know, I found out that when a guy's in prison they say: 'He's doin' bird'. D'ya know, that means 'He's doin' time' because it rhymes with 'birdlime'. D'ya get that?"

The bodyguards didn't understand it, but they laughed all the same.

"And what was that about the early bird?", Stud asked, looking at his bodyguards. They looked at each other with blank faces until one of them said: "Hey, chief, we can find out for ya".

"Just relax and shut ya face willya, do me a favor".

Stud turned to Jet again. "Look Buddy, we want ya to keep an eye on that there Gatwick. This guy's dangerous. I'm worried about this club he started: Freedom for Bears Club. That's gotta be a suspect organisation. There's only one kinda freedom, and that's our kinda freedom. Got that? Ya'know this here Gatwick guy wants to put funny ideas into bears' heads. Now listen here; me, Bird Dog, Red-tailed Hawk and Sammy here, really want ya to be our friend. All ya gotta do is keep an eye on that there Gatwick and tell us what he's up to. Be nice to him, handle him right. Sam here will come and look for ya and bring intelligence back to me. All ya gotta do is tell us his movements and what his intentions are. Ya got that?"

Well, Jet could hardly disagree. He just wanted to get out of this place.

"Yes, I've understood perfectly. If that's what you want, then I'll do it", Jet answered.

"You never had a choice, chuck. Sammy'll staple a micro-chip to ya tail, so that we know exactly where ya are all the time. Ya a wise guy. Ya don't wanna get caught up in them Red-tailed Hawk's claws. We got a deal. Now, go into downtown Lugano. The last time we checked him out, Gatwick was about to land at Lugano City Airport. Here, take this camera. Get us some shots of this Gatwick guy. Now get outta my sight".

Jet left, ready to carry out his mission.

9 Stud and Bird Dog

Sam told Stud that Bird Dog wanted to see him.

"Send him up", shouted Stud. "Ah, Bird Dog, what chicken nugget d'ya have for me?"

"I just wanted to like update ya on the Gatwick case, sir. I gotta email from Miss Acid".

"Ah, that Miss Acid! One hellava lady! They don't make 'em like that any more. Come on, what's she say".

"Miss Acid wrote that she had first seen Gatwick Bear in Gatwick Airport last Thursday, in the morning, sir. At first she thought he was a passenger, but then she thought he was a tramp lookin' to get outta the rain. Now, if he was just homeless he wouldn't, like, go back there. He'd go to the subway or somethin'. But, he hangs about that there airport. The next day, he was captured on CCTV in disguise, wearing dark glasses and fake sideburns. He was up to somethin', for sure. Miss Acid found out that he'd been sleepin' in the broom cupboard. When she went to check it out, she found plans for blowing up the airport. There was a map of the airport and five symbols, mushroom-like, y'know, like bomb explosions. One was set to go off under a table at the coffee shop, then another three in different bins around the airport. Then she spotted him..."

"That leaves another one, you dumb head", Stud interrupted.

Bird Dog counted them on his claws.

"Oh, yeah, sorry, sir, the other one was on a seat in departures. Then she spotted him airside wanting to leave the country. She tried to stop him, but he got away. Miss Acid can't make this out. But, as we know, he's in Switzerland now".

"Yeah, and that dumb head of a raven is gonna report to us. If somethin' goes wrong, we kill him".

"Who will we kill, the raven or Gatwick, sir?", Bird Dog asked.

"Both of 'em, of course, you stupid or somethin'? Where's this place of Lugano, anyway?"

"We looked it up on google earth, sir. It's south of the Alps and they speak Italian there, sir".

"Italian!! Are you crazy? They speak Italian in Italy, and Swiss in Switzerland. Sometimes, I wonder if you're up to this. I wanna know about bombs. Any sign of 'em out there in London?"

"No, sir. Miss Acid thinks that he's gone to Switzerland to recruit other terrorists and to withdraw money from a Swiss bank account to finance his evil doings, sir".

"What a woman! She's just brilliant. These English matrons are a step above the rest, I tell ya!"

"Yeah, sir, I'm sure they are".

"Focus on the job, will ya? Let me know when there's some news. Get outta my sight now and close the door behind you".

"Yes, sir".

10 Lugano City Airport

Gatwick had never been so excited in all his life. He had flown on a plane, won the lottery, met his little sister, and had got all that attention. What else could a cub want? Once he had read an article in The Guardian saying that winning the lottery didn't make you happy at all. It made you feel sad as if your life was pointless – you had no direction – and it made you feel guilty about getting money for nothing. But Gatwick felt none of that. He was absolutely gob-smacked exhilarated, never been so happy to be alive.

So trundling his big box on wheels, tied up with red rope with his left paw, and carrying his small blue Edwardian case, with rusty catches and an even rustier big lock, in his right paw, he made his way to the arrivals hall. His little sister was sitting on a big red suitcase parked near the toilets. "I must speak to her now that she's alone", Gatwick thought.

"Hello. I've been thinking about you. I've been thinking that you must be my little sister", Gatwick summoned up the courage to say.

"How do you know that?"

"Well, I don't have a family, so I must have lost it, or my family lost me. That is, a family is made up of parents and cubs. I'm a cub, you're a cub. You are on your own, and so am I. You are smaller than me, and you're female, so logic tells me that you must be my little sister. I'm Gatwick".

"Thank you, Gatwick. What you have just said is so true. Now that you've told me, I know who I am. I'm Little Sister". She liked the sound of that.

"Little Sister, I want to free you. Why don't we go off together? Why don't you join the Freedom for Bears Club? You know, you don't have to spend the rest of your life on a dusty bookshelf in a little girl's bedroom, while she goes out to play and has fun with her friends. Don't you see you are treated like an object?"

Little Sister thought how true this was. She turned her head to see if the family she belonged to were coming out of the toilets. No, they were still in there.

"All right, Gatwick, if you are my big brother, I want to be with you. You're right, I've been a doormat all my life".

"Of course, we can look after each other. Jump into my box and hide in there". Gatwick parked his small blue Edwardian case, with rusty catches and an even rustier big lock, on the floor, untied the red rope around his big box on wheels, and let Little Sister jump in. He quickly tied the box up again.

Gatwick trundled Little Sister to the information desk. He wanted to enquire about Jet before taking the bus to the city.

"Excuse me, Miss, have you seen a jet black raven called Jet who flies like a jet?"

"I don't think so. I will ask my colleague. Maria, have you seen a jet black raven called Jet who flies like a jet? No, sorry, she hasn't seen Jet, either".

Gatwick waited a while: "He might get here soon", he thought. He waited and waited, but his friend didn't turn up. As he trundled Little Sister out of the airport, Gatwick saw some brochures. He took a handful and made his way to the bus. First they would go down to the city.

But, Jet had arrived and, from his hiding place, had seen Little Sister get into Gatwick's box. He followed them out of the airport.

Gatwick stood at the bus stop and studied the timetable. There were lots of numbers above ten. Scratching his head in confusion, he thought: 'Mmmm, maybe I should just wait for the bus to turn up'. The bus soon came along. When Gatwick tried to get the box up the steps, he found he couldn't manage it – Little Sister was heavier than she looked. The bus driver stepped down to help him.

"Mamma mia, that'sa heavy. What hava you got in der, many brick?"

"No, I've got a fishing rod, a pencil sharpener, and my Little Sister".

Gatwick held out the silver shilling to pay for his fare.

"Oh, you are so simpatico. I take you free because you maka me laugh such much".

Gatwick had forgotten to tell him that he also had a cheque for £20,000 in there, but never mind, it was too late to tell him now. The driver was still laughing. When they arrived in the city centre, the driver helped Gatwick down the steps with the box.

"Excuse me. Could you tell me where there's a bank?"

"Oh, you are so simpatico. In Lugano much bank, much bank. More bank in Lugano than light in the street. You go, you see bank".

It was true. As soon as Gatwick turned around he saw a bank. But before he cashed his cheque, he wanted to let Little Sister out of the box. He carefully untied the knot and opened the box. He peered into the box. Little Sister sprang out as chuffed as can be. She would have crashed into his round head, if he hadn't been quick to get out of the way:

"Oh, it was so hot in there, Gatwick. I thought I was going to die".

"Don't be silly Little Sister, you were only born a few years ago. You're too young to die. Put all those nasty thoughts out of your mind. Let's enjoy ourselves".

"Of course, I will, Gatwick". Little Sister saw a handbag shop. "Oh, Gatwick, please, please, please, will you buy me a handbag?"

"You know I will. It's just that we've got to go to the bank first to get some money".

So Little Sister and Gatwick crossed the road. They were good cubs. When the little green man appeared on the lights, they walked across. A big white van was parked on that side of the road and the bears had to walk round it to get into the bank. There were roadworks, some men were digging a huge hole and laying cables. Gatwick strolled into the bank with Little Sister trailing after him. Jet had followed them into the bank and swooped down behind a plant where, hiding amongst the leaves, he had a direct line of sight to the cashiers. Little Sister lolled in an armchair and admired the pictures in a magazine, while she was waiting for Gatwick.

"Good afternoon, Mr. Cashier. I won a lot of money scratching a card with my wooden spoon on my flight here. The flight attendant gave me this piece of paper. She told me I could swap it for a lot of money in a bank".

"I see. I needa to check this and will be backa in a minute".

Jet couldn't understand what was happening. He had never been in a bank before. In fact, he didn't even know it was a bank, neither did he know what a bank was. But, he had to have something to tell the Eagles otherwise they would get nasty. The cashier came back.

"Sorry to keepa you waiting, sir. I hada to talk to the manager".

His phone rang. He kept saying: "Yes..., no..., yes..., no... Excuse me sir, we suggest thata you investa some of your money with us. We have some very interesting deals for you. We coulda make your money work for you".

Gatwick didn't know what he was talking about. He blinked three times, then said:

45

"Could I have the money, please?"

"Well, if you insista, sir; but I musta warn you thata going around with £20,000 in cash is not gooda. You mighta lose it. Woulda you like your money in pounds or francs?" the cashier asked.

Gatwick didn't know, so he shouted across the bank to see what Little Sister thought: "Do we want the money in pounds or francs?"

"Half and half", she answered.

"Half and half", Gatwick repeated to the cashier.

The cashier started counting the money out, and placed it in wads on the counter. Each wad had an elastic band stretched around it. Gatwick opened his box, moved the fishing rod to one side, then started placing the money neatly in rows in his box. He'd always been neat. First, the pounds; and then the francs on top. Gatwick thanked the cashier very much for giving him all that money. His box was now quite heavy, luckily it had wheels and Little Sister helped pull it along.

11 Shopping

Little Sister hadn't forgotten about the bag shop. So that was their next stop. There were so many different kinds of handbags in the shop. Gatwick wondered why they couldn't all be made in the same colour and shape. Little Sister had to touch nearly all of them. In the end, after a lot of oohing and aahing, she decided on a lime-green leather bag with four compartments, two zips and two shoulder straps. But, then... her eyes fell on the suitcases. The shop assistant came to the rescue:

"Would you like me to show you a few?" she asked in perfect English.

"Oh, you are English?", Little Sister said. "Yes, please, I'd love to see that one over there".

"Now, this one is the latest model. It's a luxury Smartmite made of very tough ABS material. It comes in pink with silver trim and has two combination locks, which makes it the most secure suitcase ever made. It has a push-pull handle at the side and moves very smoothly and easily. It has four wheels, three gears and two brakes, which are activated by treading on this pedal at the bottom of the case. I have one of these myself, and this is the last one we have in stock. We sold the others in just a few days". Little Sister was so lucky, she had to have it. She was without words. Never had she seen such a beautiful object. "And, when you open the suitcase, it plays music. You can have any ring-tone you like". Well, that did it for Gatwick: "What about *Knees Up Mother Brown*", he suggested. Little Sister and the shop-assistant agreed. That was a splendid idea.

Gatwick undid the red rope around his box and asked the lady how many notes she wanted. Five of those with 100 written on them, please. That was all right; Gatwick could count to five. In exchange, he received a small coin back, which he tossed into his box. It was so good to see Little Sister happy. With her lime-green leather handbag and pink ABS suitcase, she looked very stylish walking down the most fashionable road in Lugano City.

"Now it's your turn to buy something", she giggled.

It wasn't long before Gatwick was attracted by a shop window with an amazing variety of chocolates on show. "Wow! What a feast!" So they went in. Gatwick was sorry that all the chocolates in the shop couldn't fit into his box. So, he asked if he could have ten boxes of chocolates. That was the most he could have because he didn't know what the number after ten was. The shop assistant started filling the shiny gold boxes with the finest, exquisite, hand-crafted chocolates giving him a mixture of: truffles, pralines, chocolate covered walnuts, nougat, marzipan, Turkish delight, exotic creams, and coffee and mint creams; but, no liqueurs because they were only cubs. She gave them a big heart-shaped chocolate free of charge. She said she wanted two of those big notes. All the boxes went into a carrier bag. The two cubs walked back down the road eating the heart-shaped chocolate, truly satisfied with themselves. What a day it had been!

12 The Accident

As they walked past the bank, Gatwick, not looking where he was going (and still thinking about those tasty chocolates) stumbled on the kerb, tripped over himself and fell head first straight into the hole, along with his big box on wheels, tied up with red rope, and his small blue Edwardian case, with rusty catches and an even rustier big lock, and the chocolates. Little Sister looked into the hole, and couldn't see anything except for his paws waving around. She looked at the men in the white van with imploring watery eyes, but they were so heartless that they zoomed away. There were all kinds of pipes and cables down there, and they went all the way down the tunnel. But, Gatwick had now turned himself right way up. He came to his senses and was quite all right, apart from losing a bit of fur from the top of his head – but that would grow back with time.

Gatwick put his finger on his chin and thought, while Little Sister kept crying.

"Look, Little Sister, it's no good crying, you've got to get me out of here. Lie down on your tummy at the edge of the hole and dangle your arms down".

Little Sister did as she was asked. She would do anything to help her big brother.

"OK, Little Sister, I'll hold the fishing rod up for you to get. Can you reach it?"

"Yes, I've got it. What do I do now?"

"There's a yellow handle on the side of a little red wheel, just keep turning that. I'm going to hook things on it and you'll pull them up".

Gatwick hooked his big box on wheels, tied up with red rope, onto the fishing rod, then asked Little Sister to pull it up. There, that was one.

"Now unwind it by turning the wheel the other way".

Gatwick hooked his small blue Edwardian case, with rusty catches and an even rustier big lock, to it. Then, they did the same thing all over again with the chocolates. And, the last time round, Gatwick pushed the hook through the back of his waistcoat and was slowly hoisted up by Little Sister. She was stronger than she looked. Didn't they do well?

Now, Gatwick thought they should sort their luggage out. So they sat, with their back against the bank's wall, and started taking the boxes of chocolates out of the carrier bag.

"Let's put them in your suitcase, Little Sister".

Little Sister opened her suitcase to the tune of *Knees Up Mother Brown*.

"Yes, let's put them in my suitcase", she answered.

And that's what they did.

Gatwick had taken two beautiful chocolates, wrapped in golden crinkled foil, out of one of the boxes as a special treat for Little Sister.

"I'm very proud of you. You saved my life", he said tenderly giving her the chocolates.

"Thank you so much Gatwick, you know I'd do anything for you", she munched the chocolate truffles and handed him the wrappers.

Gatwick thought he saw a security woman. He became very frightened because she reminded him of Miss Acid:

"Quick, Little Sister, we've got to run as fast as our furry legs will take us. Quick! Run for your life".

Little Sister shot up as fast as can be and started to flee while Gatwick followed dropping the wrappers on the pavement. They hid behind the corner of a building. Little Sister stuck her head round and assured Gatwick that they were now safe. The woman was marching back in the opposite direction.

"But you dropped the wrappers, Gatwick!"

"What could I do, I'm so sorry".

"Gatwick you know very well that dropping litter is loutish behaviour. The little girl I belonged to, who was very well-behaved, used to say that those who dropped litter were not 'civilised'. I don't know what it means exactly. I only know that being 'civilised' is good, very good. And, you are not civilised now".

She started crying because she so wanted a brother who was civilised. Gatwick felt very bad. Little Sister made him feel guilty.

She went on: "I think that being civilised means that you always do the right thing. Doing the wrong thing means that you will go to jail. Gatwick, I believe you could go to jail because you dropped litter".

Now Gatwick was really worried. He murmured: "Little Sister, I promise you that I will never ever drop litter again, and that I will always take it with me until I see a bin. You're right. Everybody at Gatwick Airport is very civilised, they place their litter in bins. I hope you will forgive me this time. I don't think anyone saw me. Really, I'll never do it again".

As they walked down the road, Gatwick was overcome with guilt and shame. Never again. Little Sister eventually stopped crying.

13 Jet the Spy

Jet had watched all this from a roof top of a house on the opposite side of the road. He didn't know whether to go down and speak to Gatwick or not. As Jet was thinking about this, Sam the Eagle swooped down and landed next to him.

"Hey, man, kinda neat place you got here. What's up?"

Jet started telling Sam what he'd seen:

"When Gatwick arrived at the airport he met up with another bear. A white female with a cherry-red, heart-shaped nose. She jumped into his box, then they took the bus to Lugano City. He let her out of the box, then went into a bank where they withdrew lots of money".

"Hey, man, how much money?" Sam asked.

"Well, I don't know. I couldn't count it. But, there were wads and wads of money – really lots".

"Sounds like big bucks to me".

"Yes, well, they put this money in Gatwick's box. Next they went to buy a handbag and a suitcase, for the white bear".

"Can you describe the handbag and suitcase?"

"Oh, yes, I saw it all. The handbag is a lime-green leather bag with four compartments, two zips and two shoulder straps. Now, the suitcase is special, it's the latest model. It's a luxury Smartmite made of very tough ABS material. It's pink with silver trim and has two combination locks, a top security case..."

"A top security case, eh? I wonder what they're gonna put in that. Go on, man".

"It has a push-pull handle at the side and moves very smoothly and easily. It has four wheels, three gears and brakes, which are activated by treading on the pedal at the bottom of the case. I wish I had one of them myself, but it was the last one they had in stock. The little white bear was without words. Never had she seen such a beautiful object. And, when you open the suitcase, it plays music. You can have any ring-tone you like. They chose *Knees Up Mother Brown*".

"*Knees Up Mother Brown*, eh? Must be some code behind that. But, we'll crack it, you can bet ya bottom dollar. What did they do after that?"

"Then they went into a sweet shop to buy chocolates. Then something strange happened. I was perched here and watching them when a big white van blocked my view. When it moved out of the way, the next thing I saw was Gatwick down a big hole and the little white bear lying on her belly, arms dangling into the pit. Gatwick started hooking bags and boxes, and finally himself, to a fishing rod operated by the little white bear".

"So she was fishing all these containers out, very suspect", Sam squawked. Jet nodded in agreement.

Jet continued: "Then they sat down and put all these gold bars into the little white bear's new suitcase".

"Well, what d'ya know! Recruitin' terrorists and financing terrorist activities. Wait till I tell Bird Dog. Great work, man. See ya around".

With that he flew off, anxious to report all this new information to Stud and Bird Dog.

14 Lugano City News

The next day the following article was splattered over the front page of the Lugano City News:

RECORD BANK ROBBERY IN LUGANO CITY!

Thieves in Lugano City have stolen up to 75 million francs, in cash and gold bars, after tunnelling into a bank in what police say could be Switzerland's biggest bank heist

A 200m long tunnel into the bank was dug from the pavement by workmen carrying out roadworks. It seems that thieves took advantage of this ready-made route straight into the bank vaults. Witnesses stated that they did not know how many men had been working on the site.

It is not clear when the theft happened. The robbery was not discovered until Monday morning when the post girl opened the offices after the weekend break, so it must have happened sometime during the week before.

Neighbours revealed to reporters that van loads of material were removed each day. "They've been digging there for three months", said one witness.

The Chief Inspector told the news agency: "Some gang must have taken advantage of the roadworks. This was a sophisticated gang with expert knowledge. It's clear that they used hi-tech equipment to get the haul out. Our police force is inspecting CCTV footage from cameras placed in the area all around the bank, including rooftops nearby. We believe vital information will come from the footage. Also, the forensic department of the federal police bureau are hard at work".

The spokesperson for the bank declared that the value of the stolen bank notes and gold bars had not been determined exactly. However, sources rumoured the heist may have been the biggest bank robbery in Switzerland's history. The gang worked with talcum powder to make fingerprinting difficult. Before the robbers left the vaults, they sprayed: "Catch us if you can" on the walls.

15 Stud and Bird Dog Again

Sam reported everything that Jet had seen back to Stud.

"Hey, tell Bird Dog to get on up here. I need to tell him what to do next", Stud ordered Sam.

Bird Dog got into the lift right away and went up to Stud.

"Come on in. We've had some interestin' developments here in that Gatwick guy's case. Ya wouldn't guess what he's been up to. Wait till I tell ya. Listen here..."

So, Stud told Bird Dog the whole story.

"Gee, that's some mighty development, sir: recruitin' terrorists and financin' his activities in illicit ways. Ya mean to say like, he carried out a bank robbery with his accomplice? We gotta work out a plan here".

"We've gotta get that box, see what's in that there thing. That Gatwick guy is just a low-level player. We gotta get to the bottom of this. We can't kidnap him yet, we needa see where he leads us, see who he's workin' for. Well, what d'ya know? Who would've guessed he was such a smart nut?", Stud said shaking his head.

"Sir, I think we gotta get that box, without Gatwick realisin' we got it, otherwise we lay ourselves open. Then we won't be able to get to the high-level players", Bird Dog suggested.

"Knock it off, willya? How the hella ya gonna do that, you big dumb head!" Stud shouted.

"Hold on, sir, it's no good freakin' out. Why don't we make a box exactly like the one he's got there and then swap 'em over?"

"Hey, keep knocking", Stud ordered enthusiastically.

"Yea, we get Sam to fill our box with paper and get him to take it to Jet. When the Gatwick fella abandons his box for a moment, we change 'em over. We've gotta picture of the box. That raven's so good at aerial shots. All we gotta do is make a copy".

"Great, ya a hellava smart guy. I give ya permission to carry that out. Keep me posted".

"Yes, sir", and with that Bird Dog moved towards the door, walking backwards in case Stud threw anything at him on his way out.

16 Lugano City Airport Again

After nearly losing all their chocolate down the hole, Gatwick and Little Sister took the bus back to Lugano City Airport. Gatwick had told Little Sister that airports were good places to sleep in; they were clean, warm, safe and shiny. And, what's more they had muffins. But, Gatwick didn't really feel like eating muffins now. He had just finished off the box of chocolates with Little Sister. They were feeling weezy, or was it woozy? Whichever, that's how they felt.

They got back on the airport bus. The driver was so pleased to see Gatwick again.

"Hello, my friend. So you got you a girl now". You a coola operator as they say in the song.

Gatwick didn't know the song, he only knew *Knees Up Mother Brown*.

The bus driver continued: "I'll help you with thata box, it's such heavy, with your fishing rod and your little sister in there. Oh, you are so simpatico".

Gatwick took a bank note out of his box and gave it to the driver. When Gatwick opened the box, the driver saw that it was full of money.

"Hey, you didn't tell me you hada all thata money in there. I think you poor bear".

"I won a lot of money by scratching a card with my wooden spoon", Gatwick explained.

"Hey, you thinka I stupid or something", the driver got red in the face with anger.

"Sorry, I didn't mean to offend you. Really, I didn't".

Little Sister didn't like this man's attitude. It was no way to speak to her big brother.

"Well, this time you pay. You pay for you, for your friend and for every bag you have!"

Gatwick didn't mind. The thought of not paying never came into his mind. Gatwick handed the banknote over to the driver and, at last, they set off for the airport. The bus swung round the bends and, as it did, Gatwick and Little Sister held on tight and felt even more weezy, or was it woozy? Anyway, they probably felt both by now. On arrival, the driver folded his arms on his big pot belly and didn't lift a finger to help them with their luggage. So Gatwick and Little Sister took one piece down at a time, Gatwick holding one end and Little Sister the other. They thanked the driver very much, then headed for departures. There they sat, on a hard bench, watching people go by and, nearly without realising it, they munched their way through yet another box of chocolates between them. Night started falling and all the flights for the day had left. The airport became very still, quiet and a security man started switching the lights off. He noticed the two cubs and walked over to them saying:

"I'm so sorry, but you have to leave. The airport is shutting down for the night".

Gatwick couldn't believe the furry ears on his round head. Gatwick Airport never closed! Would they have to sleep outside?

"There's an excellent airport hotel, two minutes on foot from here. It's a five-star: the Grand Hotel. Come with me, I'll show you which way to go".

So, Gatwick and Little Sister followed him out of the airport and waddled down the path towards the hotel following the man's directions. The bears didn't even know that hotels existed, let alone one as nice as this. The two furry creatures couldn't believe their eyes. The entrance doors were of glass and rimmed with gold, they slid open automatically to welcome the bears in. Gatwick and Little Sister found themselves standing in a spacious entrance hall. They stood in the middle of the hall and threw their heads backwards to look up at the gigantic crystal chandelier sparkling over them. The oh-so-polished floor they were standing on was in beautiful Italian marble. And, in the middle of the huge reception area was a lively fountain with water shooting up and breaking up into transparent drops as it danced into the silvery pool. A man was smiling at them from behind the shiny wood-panelled reception desk:

"Good evening, sir; good evening, madam. How can I help you?" he said.

Gatwick told the man that they had just come from Lugano City Airport. The security man there had directed them to this hotel. They needed somewhere to stay for the night.

"Then you have come to the right place", the man answered. "We have an indoor swimming pool, an award-winning restaurant, as well as an American grill room. Each room is hand decorated. Would you like a suite?"

Well that was music to Gatwick's ears. He'd stopped feeling sick. Of course, he'd like a sweet. Little Sister said she'd like one, too.

"We only have one free: the roof-garden suite. You can share it. It splits into two quite well", he assured them.

They thought that sharing a sweet would be fine. Though they weren't sure what a roof-garden sweet looked like or what flavour it was.

"Could you describe it to us, please?" Little Sister asked.

"It's beautiful and extremely elegant in soothing pastel shades and covered in richly coloured layers of fabric. Very cool in summer and warm in winter. Everyone enjoys it very much – it's a memorable experience".

Both together the bears shouted: "We'll have it!".

The receptionist continued: "The room has a view looking out onto the mountains and landscaped Italian sunken gardens. There are two en suite bathrooms with an en suite jacuzzi, small living room, four-poster beds with brass fittings and water mattresses, flat-screen TV..."

"That's OK", interrupted Gatwick, getting bored with the list. "We don't mind what's in it. We only want a place to sleep for the night because we got thrown out of the airport. So we don't mind what it's like".

"Ah, and if you decide to extend your stay, you will receive a ten percent discount". Gatwick knew what 'ten' was, but he had no idea what 'percent' meant – maybe they were sweets, too! The receptionist, still smiling, gave them a key each and signalled the porter to carry their cases up. They went up in the mirrored lift and stepped out into the plush corridor when the doors opened to the sound of 'ding'. Down the corridor they stomped until they came to a polished wooden door with golden knocker and handle.

In the meantime, the bus driver had arrived home to his wife. "What hava you made for me, my bella?" he asked his wife, recognising the smell of pasta bolognese wafting in from the kitchen.

"Pasta bolognese, amore mio. Mada wida my own handsa", she answered, as she wiped her hands on her apron.

"Thatsa what I like", he said to please her.

"Dida you hear about de robbery today at the banka?

"No, tell me whata happened".

"Looka here, you canna read in de Lugano City News", she said thrusting the paper under his nose.

"Oh, mamma mia, I know who dida dis. It wasa dose bear I took to de airport! He only hada silva shillin when he arrive and hada full box ofa money and a girl when he went!"

"Oh, mamma mia, mamma mia", shouted his wife. "You musta calla de polis this minute".

She passed him the phone. The police had shut down for the night. He'd phone them first thing in the morning, when he got up for his late shift at 11 o'clock, and tell them everything he knew.

17 Five-star Life

Gatwick and Little Sister were busy making themselves comfortable in their suite. Little Sister went through all the trinkets in the bathroom. She put on the plastic shower cap, then went and sat on the water bed and started playing around with the remote control. Gatwick was having fun trying to work out which light switch turned on which light. When he had understood that, he started tampering with the air-conditioning. "Is the air all right for you Little Sister, or would you like it cooler?" asked the ever-considerate Gatwick.

Little Sister was watching Strictly Come Dancing. Oh, she did like those gowns. And, she just adored the way the dancers twirled and swirled about, so elegant and light-footed. Gatwick was still fiddling about with the air-conditioning. He thought he'd give up because, whatever he did, it didn't seem to make any difference to the room temperature. So he tried opening the safe he'd found in one of the wardrobes. He pressed his ear against the dial and heard it clicking. He liked the sound. So he kept turning the dial backwards and forwards going faster and faster... until he heard a loud click of the lock and the safe sprang open.

"Oh, look, Little Sister there are some sparkling little stones in this box".

"Let me have a look", she answered, a little irritated for having been interrupted while watching TV. "Mmm, very nice", she said as she watched them twinkle in her paws. The stones were strung together in a round shape.

"I think you're supposed to put it around your neck. Miss Acid wore one which looked as if it was made of animals' teeth". With the help of Gatwick, Little Sister put on the diamond necklace and went back to watching TV.

Then, Gatwick had an idea:

"Why don't we go down to the swimming pool?"

"Wow! Yes, let's go swimming", shouted Little Sister in glee.

So they got into the lift and went down. The pool was so big and blue. There was no-one else in it. They had it all to themselves! Gatwick went up the steps of the long slide. It was so high, it made him dizzy. He sat down and slid into the pool going "Whee!" all the way. He liked that and thought he'd do it all over again. After that, he tried the trampoline – that was even more fun. Little Sister, more cautious than Gatwick, took the steps into the pool one by one and backwards, but only after she'd put a paw in the water to test the temperature. Well, they had such fun splashing each other and diving and putting their heads under the water. They had got themselves very wet indeed. "Maybe we ought to go and dry out" Little Sister suggested to Gatwick, looking at his drenched waistcoat and fur.

"Yes, let's go up and see if we can get the hairdryers to work", said Gatwick.

When they had blow dried themselves, after much messing around with the hairdryers, Little Sister thought it might be a swell idea to have some more chocolates. So, they had another box between them, and then each rolled over onto their own water bed, feeling well and truly sick, and fell asleep.

Early next morning, Jet was looking for worms in the hotel's landscaped garden. The bears were sitting on loungers on their balcony basking in the sun and having breakfast. They were having oak-smoked kippers, sliced – smoked Scottish salmon and Russian caviar, as well as warm butter cakes with lots of honey and marmalade, washing it all down with hot chocolate. The Red Vultures on the terrace next to them were having a similar breakfast, but they were drinking vodka instead of chocolate. All of a sudden Gatwick shouted out: "Jet!".

Little Sister wondered why Gatwick should be so surprised. After all, they were near an airport.

"No, you don't understand. It's my best friend, my best friend: Jet the Raven from Gatwick Airport! Jet! Jet!"

Jet turned around and looked up at the roof-garden. Oh, no, Gatwick had seen him. What now?

"Oh, watcha, Gatwick. How are you? Fancy meeting you here of all places".

"How come you're here? Have you just arrived? You know, I looked for you at the airport when I got here. I was so worried about you because I thought something really horrible had happened to you. From the plane, I saw how those nasty Eagles were knocking you about. I've been so, so worried".

"Look, I'm OK, mate. Don't worry I'm fine. Yes, well, they did peck at me quite a bit, then they let me go and, but hey, I'm fine now".

"Well, what are you doing here?" Gatwick asked.

"I was waiting for you 'cause I knew you'd be coming back this way, see!"

Gatwick was a softy and was touched by Jet's concern. "Come up here and meet my little sister".

In one curved swoop, Jet flew up to the bears' balcony. Gatwick introduced Jet and Little Sister to each other, and Jet joined the bears for breakfast. Jet didn't like fish, but he certainly adored the butter cakes that Gatwick had crumbled up for him. What a splendid way to start a day, with your Little Sister and your best friend.

"So, what are you two going to do today?" Jet asked.

"We're going up mountains and having a picnic. I want to fish in the lakes up there, and Little Sister wants to sunbathe. You can join us, if you like". The staff at the hotel had filled a wicker basket with a tasty picnic for them.

Jet said that he'd love to, but that he couldn't possibly because he had other plans. Then Jet asked which mountain they'd be going up.

"Monte Generoso, but it's known as Emerald Mountain", replied Little Sister. "It's ever such a big, big mountain – high and wide. I'm so excited!"

It wouldn't be difficult for Jet to get there before them. He was agile and could fly – bears were always so slow getting anywhere.

"By the way", Jet really had to ask this question, "how can you afford to stay in a place like this? Not exactly like living at Gatwick Airport, is it?"

Gatwick replied: "You wouldn't believe it, if I told you".

"Try me", said Jet.

"It was by scratching a card with my wooden spoon, and all this money was under it".

"You're right, Gatwick, you know. I don't believe you. And what about your 'little sister', did you plan to meet her here?

"Oh, no, we met by chance, we just happened to be on the same plane".

'Another fine tale', Jet thought. "I'll have to love you and leave you, I'm afraid; got masses to do. Thanks for the breakfast, those cakes were really something else".

Jet had found out about their plans for the day. Later that morning, Sam would be coming back to give Jet instructions. At least, he would have something to tell Sam, which meant not being bullied by the Eagles. As promised, Sam arrived on the dot.

"Hiya, man. Big chief says you gotta get Gatwick's box. We gotta know what he's carryin' around in there. Could be anythin'! Now don't go shopping him to the Swiss police. We don't want 'em bangin' him up for robbery when we got bigger issues on our claws – the lives of thousands of innocent freedom loving, law abiding citizens are at stake. We gotta protect our people. That's our mission".

18 End of Five-star Life

Gatwick and Little Sister had finished breakfast and were sitting on their water beds sorting their luggage out. One of the wheels of Gatwick's big box on wheels, tied up with red rope, had come off. Oh, dear, he didn't know how to fix it. Both he and Little Sister fiddled around with the wheel and finally managed to fix it back on again, although still a bit wobbly.

Little Sister smiled. She'd just had a wonderful idea: "Why don't we take everything out of our luggage and then put everything back in again?"

"I did think of that, too", replied Gatwick, wondering how come she always came up with these good ideas before him. "It's surprising how much you can get into boxes, cases and handbags, if you pack them carefully. Let's put the money in your suitcase, Little Sister, under the boxes of chocolate". They had seven boxes left. "Why don't we share another box of chocolates now?"

Little Sister thought that an excellent idea.

So they sat there, with all the piles of money around them, and ate their way through another box of chocolates. Now there were six left. Good Little Sister started packing her suitcase to the tune of *Knees Up Mother Brown*. The wads of pounds first – those were to go at the bottom of her suitcase – then the boxes of chocolates, and the Swiss francs on top. Like Gatwick, she was so neat and tidy. Now for the wooden spoon, the fishing rod and the pencil sharpener. Those would go in Gatwick's Edwardian case with rusty catches and an even rustier big lock, while Little Sister would look after his sunglasses and fake sideburns by placing them in her new lime-green leather handbag with four compartments. She decided to keep her necklace on because she adored the way it glittered. Now for the picnic.

"Let's put the picnic in your box, Gatwick", Little Sister suggested. "We can take the food and drink out of the wicker basket, put it all in your box and leave the wicker basket here. That way, we won't have the extra weight, and the box will get lighter and lighter through the day".

So, that's what they did. Again, Gatwick wondered why he hadn't had that good idea.

The two of them went down to reception to pay their bill.

"Did you have a pleasant stay?", the receptionist asked, gawking at Little Sister's diamond necklace.

"Oh, it was lovely, thank you. We enjoyed ourselves very much. How many notes would you like?", Gatwick asked.

"Here's your bill. That's one thousand francs please".

"Sorry, could you repeat that please?"

Gatwick didn't know how much one thousand francs were. He looked at Little Sister for help, but her face was blank, she didn't know either.

Little Sister opened her suitcase and showed him the money. Perched on the reception desk was one of the Red Vultures who had had the suite next to the bears. One of the Red Vultures, called Dazbog, had seen Jet go up to Gatwick's balcony that morning. He knew Jet was working for the Eagles, and the Eagles were the most hated enemy of the Red Vultures. Gatwick and Little Sister must be working for the Eagles. Dazbog was gob smacked when he saw all that money. OK, so he had seen a lot of money in his life. But never had he seen it all laid out like that: in a suitcase to the tune of *Knees Up Mother Brown*. And, he could see the shiny gold peeping out between the notes.

"How many of these would you like?" Gatwick asked the receptionist.

"Ten, please".

Slowly counting to ten, Gatwick placed the notes on the counter.

"That's lovely. Thank you so much".

While Little Sister shut her suitcase, Gatwick asked the receptionist if he would get them a taxi. That bus driver was so rude, Gatwick was not taking the bus any more. The receptionist wanted to know where the taxi should take them:

"To the little train at the foot of Emerald Mountain".

"Very well, I'll do that right away. You can go and wait in the courtyard, the taxi will be here in five minutes. Thank you for choosing our hotel. I hope you had a pleasant stay and hope to see you here again soon. It was a pleasure having you. Have a safe journey. Goodbye".

The bears bid him 'goodbye'. What a friendly man he was!

Just about everyone knew the bears were going up Emerald Mountain that day.

19 The Police

The Police were making great progress in investigating the great bank robbery. A phone call from a bus driver had given them some very interesting leads. The same bears the bus driver had described were clearly seen on the CCTV footage the police had checked. Sure enough, there were the bears in front of the bank as clear as anything.

The Chief Inspector had been shown the images of Little Sister fishing the haul and Gatwick out of the hole. True, they hadn't seen Gatwick go into the hole because the big white van blocked the view. But, the police thought that if he came out of the hole, then he must have gone in – that's only logic. They also saw the bears placing gold bars into Little Sister's suitcase. The bars had been handed to the little white bear in a carrier bag and then placed in the suitcase at the scene of the crime. These criminals were audacious.

The bus driver had told the police that he had taken the bears up to the airport, that they had probably left the country and might be in Brazil by now, where they would lead a life of lazy luxury (while he had to keep driving backwards and forwards on a bus all his life. And, every evening he had to listen to that wife of his screaming at him and suffer the pinching of his cheeks – though he did love the old bat – because that's all he had).

So, that was their lead. The bus driver had taken the bears to the airport. That's where the investigation would start. The Chief Inspector went there himself. He questioned everyone. It was from the security man that he obtained the most interesting information. According to him, the bears were anxious to fly off somewhere but had missed all the flights – they were still there until after the last flight left. He had to turf them out of the airport and show them the way to the Grand Hotel:

"I really had no idea they were carrying all that money around!" the security man exclaimed. And, that was the statement that appeared on the front page of Lugano City News the next day.

The Grand Hotel was the Chief Inspector's next destination. Here, he spoke to the receptionist:

"It's true, they had a suitcase full of money and gold bars. The little white bear had a diamond necklace on, too. I saw it all with my own eyes, right here before me in the reception hall. The little white bear opened the suitcase, to the tune of *Knees Up Mother Brown*, and I saw the haul inside".

"*Knees Up Mother Brown*, you say?" the Inspector asked.

"Yes, why does that mean something?"

"There might be a code – a message of some sort – in that tune. I'll have to pass this information on to our code breakers".

"Well, what do you know!" exclaimed the receptionist, "whoever would have imagined such a thing? Real life is more incredible than in films".

"Did they give you any clues as to where they'd be going next?"

"Oh, yes we gave them a packed lunch. They were going to have a picnic on top of Emerald Mountain. I even called a taxi to take them to the railway station. From there, they were taking the train up the mountain".

"Many thanks for your help. I think we've got them now. We'll have our forces onto them in no time".

The Chief Inspector left. He hadn't noticed that Dazbog, who was sitting in an armchair in the hall hiding behind his newspaper, had overheard the whole lot.

20 Emerald Mountain

It was the most beautiful sunny day, just right for a picnic. Gatwick and Little Sister arrived at the train station at the foot of Emerald Mountain. They loaded their luggage, and themselves, on the little red mountain train on the rack-and-pinion railway. It was not long before the steam engine gave two chugs and stuttered into action. A big puff of smoke came out of its chimney. The train went diagonally over a road at a level crossing, Gatwick waved goodbye with his wooden spoon to the pedestrians standing there waiting to cross the road: "Cheerio!"

"Cheerio!", Little Sister copied her big brother.

The way soon became steep as it went through some woods. All of a sudden they were in a pitch black tunnel. The driver honked the loud horn just as the nose of the train was about to emerge from darkness.

"What did he do that for?" Little Sister asked Gatwick.

"It's because there may be some animals on the tracks. There are a lot of animals up here. I saw the pictures in the brochure. The chamois is the symbol of Emerald Mountain. Did you know that their fur is light brown in summer and dark-brown in winter? Our fur doesn't change colour, does it?"

"That is so interesting, Gatwick", she was hugely proud of her big brother. What a life she was having now. She briefly thought of the dusty book shelf, but soon put it out of her mind and admired the view, which was now breathtaking, really breathtaking. Little Sister stopped breathing, her round head turned red, and her eyes opened wide. The sheer vertical drops were awesome: frightening but exciting. Gatwick suggested that she looked down at her paws for a moment, to get herself together, while he put his arm around her shoulders to comfort her. She soon perked up, so Gatwick proceeded in telling her what other animals lived on Emerald Mountain.

"In the brochure, I also saw pictures of squirrels, goats, cows and even a brown bear".

"A brown bear!" exclaimed Little Sister.

"Yes, an enormous one. Look, Little Sister".

"My word; he's huge. Let's see if we can find him and talk to him!"

"Good idea! There's a bear cave up there, it's called Grotta dell'Orso. We'll go look for him in there. Look there are also lots of different types of birds. Hey, look at this funny woodpecker, it's red. Did you ever see a red woodpecker in your life?"

"Well, no, you don't get to see much sitting on a shelf, you know".

"Then there are owls, blackcaps, kites, wrynecks, buzzards, swallows, larks, wrens, ravens, and others I don't know the names of".

"I only know what ravens look like out of those", said Little Sister candidly.

"Well you see, owls are very wise and know a lot; blackcaps have black caps on their heads if they're male like me, and brown caps on their heads if they're female like you; kites can glide a long way; wrynecks have a dark line running down their backs from their necks; flying buzzards hold their wings up like a V; swallows have long tail streamers; larks get up early in the morning; and wrens are a bit dumpy, like us".

"Gatwick, you're so intelligent. How do you know so much?"

"Once a passenger left a birdwatching book on a seat at Gatwick Airport, and I spent all afternoon studying it".

The small steam train slowly climbed the slopes, chugging and puffing as it went. It was now above the treeline. No trees could grow above a certain height. The higher up trees are the shorter they grow. They got shorter and shorter as the bears moved up the mountain, until there were no trees at all.

After forty minutes the train stopped and all the passengers got off. The first thing the bears did was to rush to a railing at the edge of the mountainside, press their furry noses against it, and watch the goats climbing up the mountain face. "Hello, goats!", the bears shouted down. But they didn't answer. Only one looked up quickly, a bit irritated, and then went back to eating his patch of grass. They weren't very friendly.

"Let's try the cows", Little Sister giggled. She started running towards the sound of cowbells: clang, clang; clang, clang... Swiss milk cows were taken high up in the Alps for summer grazing. They were taken up in a procession, all together like children on a school outing. These must have been the most beautiful cows in the world. They were all different: brown or black, with and without spots. Gatwick and Little Sister soon got friendly with the cows. In next to no time the two bears were using the cows' tails as swings. The cows loved it and swayed the bears to and fro as high as they could go:

"Hold on tight", shouted Gatwick with glee to Little Sister.

When they were tired of that game, Gatwick thought he would pick some flowers and place them behind the cows' ears. He ran off and came back with a small white star-shaped flower. Then he climbed onto one of the cows' backs and placed it behind her ear. She turned her head round and said:

"Youoo knowoo youoo can't pick the flowers here. It is forbidden and against the law! Moo! That is a precious edelweiss".

Gatwick was horrified and so was Little Sister. "What can I do now?", he asked, "I can't put it back. I'm so so sorry".

Little Sister started crying.

"Please don't cry Little Sister, I'll never ever do it again". It took a while for a smile to come back to Little Sister's face.

Gatwick wanted to know what the tags were on their ears. They explained that it was like a passport. The tag has the cow's name on it, the cow's date of birth, and its cow identity number: Gatwick and Little Sister went from cow to cow looking at their names: Carolina, Margherita, Celestina and Angelina.

"Swiss cows, I must tell you that you make the most delicious chocolate".

The cows answered in chorus: "Thank youoo for the compliment".

With that, the bears decided that they'd have another box of chocolates between them. To get to the boxes of chocolate, Little Sister had to take out all the Swiss francs and place them beside her on the grass. She handed the box to Gatwick, then she neatly put all the money back in again. When they'd finished the chocolates, they thought they'd start their picnic. They emptied all the goodies from Gatwick's box onto the grass. The cows joined them. What a feast!

When they were all full, Gatwick placed all the litter back in the box. He wasn't going to be accused of being a litter lout again! In fact, Gatwick cleaned the whole field. He had also seen that the cows had dropped splats of their dung on the grass. He shovelled them all up with his wooden spoon and hurled those into the box, too. Then he went back to all the laughing and rolling about in the grass with the others.

During this merry mayhem, Jet had flown down and, with one quick swoop dropped the imitation big box on wheels, tied up with red rope, onto the grass and took away the real one – as quick as a flash of lightning.

21 The Brown Bear

The cows started telling the bears about the Brown Bear who lived on Emerald Mountain. They said that some shepherds were hunting after him. They wanted to kill him before he killed their sheep. Gatwick and Little Sister were horrified. Gatwick asked how they knew the bear was there. It seemed that the shepherds had found some bear fur and bear droppings. The Brown Bear must have wandered into Switzerland from the Italian side of the Alps. Some shepherds said that they had seen it through binoculars.

It was now time for Gatwick and Little Sister to leave the cows and make their way to the Bear's Cave. The cows gave them directions. It was quite a distance but all they had to do was to follow the mountain path. On and on they trudged with their luggage. Little Sister's paws were hurting, she wanted a rest. They sat down on the grass and admired the different greens in front of them. The darkest green was formed by the reflection of a cloud between the mountain and the sun. All of a sudden Dazbog flew down with a swoosh, seized the imitation box, by hooking the red rope on to his beak, rose steeply and glided away. Gatwick was devastated. He'd had that box all his life; though, of course, he didn't realise it was an imitation. Now he was only left with his small blue Edwardian case with rusty catches and an even rustier big lock. Poor Gatwick!

They started on their journey again. There were helicopters circling over their heads everywhere. The bears enjoyed watching them. The sound of helicopters seemed to get louder. Suddenly, a deafening gun shot was heard. It was so loud that it made the bears jump, and then tremble with fright. They huddled up together, lay down on the grass against the mountain face, and held Little Sister's suitcase in front of them for protection. They waited and waited for a long time, until they were certain there was no longer any danger. They had heard no more shots and the helicopters had flown away.

The sun was going down, the evening breeze began to ruffle the bears' fur. The last train down to the valley had left. The bears had no idea how far the cave was. Neither did our bears realise how dangerous mountains were. Gatwick had only lived at Gatwick Airport and Little Sister on a shelf – they were totally clueless. They had no idea that the temperature fell sharply at night, that creatures could freeze to death. The Alps were snow-capped all the year round. Even when the temperature in the valley was scorching hot, the ice and snow still hugged the tips of the mountains.

The two bears were still marching along the mountain path until hardly a ray of light beamed from the sky. Night time had fallen by the time they finally reached the cave. They poked their heads in. It was pitch black in there. All they could do was to tread carefully, find a spot to sleep on, and hold each other's hand while they waited for the morning sun to rise. Gatwick managed to feel his way with his wooden spoon; he clung to it for good luck. Little Sister was even too scared to cry. Gatwick thought they should try and sleep where they were instead of walking further into the cave. There might be pot holes, or deep water wells, or prowling animals, or slimy reptiles, or creepy insects, or all sorts of nasties deeper in the cave. They needed to sleep and to be fresh in the morning to walk all the way back to the little train station.

So, they lay on the hard ground, side by side, trying not to let the slightest noise worry them. The clouds moving in front of the moon were projecting sinister silvery shadows through the entrance and on to the walls of the cave. Suddenly, Little Sister felt someone was lurking there, near her. She could feel a gaze on her, and thought she heard breathing. She sat up and turned around, all she saw were two white eyeballs glowing at her in the dark. Slowly, they were moving nearer towards her until they were right there in front of her. Then she felt a gentle stroke on one of her shoulders, then another stroke on her other shoulder. She was being gripped. Little Sister was petrified. A strange voice asked: "Who are you?"

Little Sister couldn't speak. So Gatwick answered: "Please don't harm us. We're only two little peaceful cubs".

"What are you doing here?", the voice continued.

"We wanted to visit this cave. We didn't realise it was so far, and arrived here when it was nearly night time. So we couldn't go back because we couldn't see our way in the dark". Gatwick found the courage to ask a question: "Are you the Brown Bear?"

"Who told you about the Brown Bear?" the voice asked back.

"We met some cows, they told us that everyone thought that the Brown Bear was on Emerald Mountain".

"I'm not the Brown Bear. He was shot and killed late this afternoon".

"Who are you then? Please tell us".

Little Sister was freed from the grip. "I'm his widow: Mother Brown".

Mother Brown had been frightened out of her skin, too. But, now she let all her feelings burst out and told the little bears her story:

"I'm an Italian bear. Gilbert moved from England to Italy when we got married. We were living peacefully and happily on the high latitudes of the Italian mountain tops. We loved nature so much: the wild flowers, the smell of the rain... During the day we would go hunting for food: nuts and berries to store away; and in the evenings we would sit together and look up at the birds and the changing colours of the sky... Then, we started roaming further, as you do. Had we known that it is illegal to cross the border, we certainly would not have come here. One mountain looked like another to us. I don't think we realised how far we walked that day. You can imagine our joy when we found this cave. Well, it was a ready-made home, somewhere we could settle down and have cubs. We didn't want to start a family until we had a cosy home".

"So, you don't have any cubs?" Gatwick asked.

"No, unfortunately, we didn't have any", Mother Brown confirmed. "As I was saying we relocated and started by doing the place up. When daylight comes, you will see how much work has gone into decorating our new den. We even built a secret extension round the back".

"But what happens when tourists visit the cave during the day? Don't they see you?"

"Oh, no! We were always out of the den when the first little train arrived in the morning, and we came back here when the last train left".

"It's a lovely location, Mother Brown", nodded Little Sister.

"Yes, well, we liked it here", Mother Brown continued. "We later found out that Swiss shepherds are very protective of their sheep. They thought we would kill their sheep. Really, they needn't have worried because we don't eat mutton or lamb. There are no protection laws for bears here. Every day they would comb the area but didn't find us, until, this afternoon..." Mother Brown started sobbing as she spoke, "until... this afternoon... we were spotted by patrols. Someone shot him and took his body away. My poor, poor, Bertie, how could they do such a thing to him? Men are so cruel, so cruel".

"We're so sorry", said the little bears together.

"Please, don't cry, Mother Brown, you've got us now", Gatwick comforted her. "You know, we don't have a mother, so we must have lost her, or she lost us. That is, a family is made up of parents and cubs. I'm a cub, and Little Sister is a cub. You don't have cubs, and we don't have a mother. So logic tells me that you must be our mother and Bertie was our father".

"Oh, Gatwick and Little Sister, this must be the saddest and happiest day in my life. I have lost a husband, but I've found two cubs to look after. Thank you, Gatwick. What you have just said is so true. Now that you've told me, I know I am your mother. Please call me 'Mama'". She liked the sound of that. "Let's get some sleep now darlings, I am so tired".

The three bears slept for a few hours. But soon, the sun started rising slowly in the distance from behind the mountains opposite. Gatwick woke up first, then he woke Little Sister and Mama. They had to leave the cave as the train would be coming up the mountain soon with its first load of tourists.

22 The Hideout

Before leaving Little Sister admired the colour scheme of Mama's interior design: lime-green and pink. What good taste Mama had! They left the cave, with what was left of their luggage. Gatwick went out first but he didn't know where to go. "We need to hide", whispered Mama Brown. "The hunters probably don't know I exist but, if someone sees me and tells them, they will be after me. I know a place where we can go. It is a hard climb, but worth it. Nobody else, apart from Bertie and I, know if its existence. Or, should I say 'knew' in the case of Bertie?" and she started sobbing again.

"Please, Mama, we love you dearly!" said Little Sister.

"And we'll look after you!" exclaimed Gatwick.

Mama cheered up a little to hear such tender enthusiasm. She went on: "It is situated in such an inaccessible place that it is not visible whether on foot or from the air. There's a little sparkling blue lake up there: Bertie's and mine – our secret lake – now it's yours too".

Gatwick could not hide his excitement. At last, he would have the chance to go fishing with his rod. He was a bit of a show off when he was fishing. He loved to have an audience, Little Sister and Mama could watch and admire him. They could go: "Ooooh", when he caught fish. With that in mind the climb didn't seem as tiring as it would have done otherwise.

It was true. The lake was simply stunning, it sparkled like Little Sister's diamonds in the morning sun. The ripples moved gently, and softly lapped against the banks. All around, they were surrounded by the deepest silence – not a whisper. The shadows on the lake and green, green mountains made gliding patterns, which Little Sister and Mama watched intently as they breathed in the freshness of the morning air and felt the warmth of the day's new sunny beams on their bodies. What delight! Gatwick had already begun fishing.

At midday, they ate a trout each, which Gatwick had caught amid much joy (and showing off). When tea-time came around, they indulged in a box of chocolates between them, followed by the berries and nuts Mama had brought up with her in her apron pocket. They were a new-found family. They were happy.

It was nearly time for the last train to go down. Mama could tell the time by the length of the shadows spreading down across the valleys. Soon all the tourists would leave; the mountains would be all theirs again. They could go back to their den. Slowly, but surely, they made their way back following Mama down the winding and dusty track. She was an expert mountaineer – only she knew the way. So many were the bends and tracks shooting off in all directions that keeping to the right pathway meant expert knowledge. Neither Gatwick nor Little Sister had any hope of remembering the way. They finally arrived back in their cave and Mama started getting dinner ready. That evening she would make blackberry crumble like she used to make for Bertie. He had loved blackberry crumble because it brought back fond memories of his native England.

Stirring was another of Gatwick's favourite activities, so he ran to get his wooden spoon because he wanted to do all the stirring that there was to do. Soon Gatwick had flour all over his head and waistcoat. Mama sent him out of the kitchen and ordered him to go out to play for a while. She would call him when it was ready.

23 Gatwick Goes Out to Play

Gatwick was fascinated by the helicopters buzzing around in the evening sky. He started jumping around waving his wooden spoon and shouting "Hello". Then, he ran and ran, trying to chase them. He had distanced himself from the cave without realising it. Where was he? Now he started getting a bit worried. But, the helicopters were coming his way; they were moving the air so much that all Gatwick's fur blew back, he nearly lost his grip on his wooden spoon as he fell over backwards. One of the helicopters landed. A man in uniform marched up to him. "Gatwick, we know it's you. Don't resist us. Drop your wooden spoon and put your paws behind your head, then get up very slowly". Gatwick did exactly as he was told. He had no idea what was happening. He had never seen these men before. What did they want? Maybe they would to take him for a ride in their helicopter. The men ordered Gatwick to get into their helicopter and to sit still. One of them picked up his wooden spoon and threw it in the helicopter. They were taking him to the police headquarters where he would be questioned by the Chief of Police. The helicopter took off in a straight line and then headed off towards the City. When they arrived, Gatwick was thrown in a cell.

Gatwick sat there with his wooden spoon for quite a long time, but nobody came. He started thinking about his Little

Sister and his Mama – how worried they'd be! And, he also started thinking about the blackberry crumble he didn't get around to eating. The eyes in his round head were watery. Little Sister said that litter louts could end up in prison because they were not civilised. She was so right.

Mama and Little Sister had finished making blackberry crumble. It had a mouth-watering light-brown sugar crust on it. Mama waited for it to cool down and then drizzled more caster sugar over it. What a finishing touch! Mama was an excellent cook: "Go and call Gatwick, will you, Little Sister. Both of you, go and wash your paws then come and have supper".

Little Sister put her head out of the cave door and shouted: "Gatwick, supper's ready! Dinner's ready!", she waited a moment for his reply. Nothing, only the silence of the brooding mountains. "Gatwick, please stop messing around. Come on!" Again, there was no answer. It was evening, and the sun had already started moving down behind the mountains opposite. Little Sister went a short way along the stony track and called again. No answer. She rushed back home, crying as she went, to tell Mama.

"Mama! Mama! I can't find Gatwick!"

"All right, now; don't panic. I'm sure he'll get back soon. He's probably just playing somewhere, hasn't realised how time has passed". But, Mama was worried. After what had happened to Bertie, she couldn't help being on edge.

"What if he's been shot, like our dad, Bertie?", Little Sister spurted out.

"Don't say such silly things. We haven't heard any shots. No, he hasn't been shot".

"Look, you stay here and don't move. I'll go further down the track, and see if I can find him".

After what seemed like an eternity, Mama came back – without Gatwick. Mama and Little Sister were too worried to eat. In fact, they were sick with worry. Mama took Little Sister into her arms, sat down, placed her on her lap, and cuddled her tight. "Everything will be all right", she said. But, night was now closing in over the mountain and creeping into the cave. Mama thought that Gatwick was surely lost. The problem was that at that altitude spending a night on the open mountains could mean freezing to death. And, Gatwick was only wearing a waistcoat, really not warm enough. Neither did he have anything to drink or eat with him.

24 Questioning

The Chief Inspector arrived and asked Gatwick if he'd like a drink.

"Could I have a fizzy drink, please?"

"Of course. Constable, can you bring us a couple of fizzy drinks, please?"

"Right you are, sir", and off the constable went.

"So, Gatwick, I suppose you know why you're here?"

"Yes, sir. I'm so sorry. I haven't been very civilised. I promise I will never ever do it again".

"Yes, well, it's a bit late for that".

"I know it was naughty. But, you can be sure that I regret it very much".

"Are you willing to sign a statement that you are guilty?"

"Yes, sir, I'm guilty. I can't hide that".

"No, you can't because we have CCTV images of you and your accomplice in front of the bank".

"Sorry, sir. What does 'accomplice' mean?

"It means that...", the constable came in with the fizzy drinks. The Chief Inspector went on: "It means that there was someone with you who helped you commit the crime".

"Oh, no, no, you can't blame Little Sister. I take all the blame, Inspector".

"So, it's your sister, is it? Keep it all in the family, eh?"

Gatwick had lost him. He didn't know what to say so didn't answer but started sipping his fizzy drink instead. The Inspector asked Gatwick if he'd like something to eat.

"Yes, please", he replied. "A tuna sandwich and ice-cream would be nice". Reference to food made Gatwick think of Mama, Little Sister and blackberry crumble. Tears came to his eyes.

"Well, it's no good crying now, is it? You should have thought about that before committing the crime", said the Inspector.

"If you let me go, I will clean up all the streets of the City".

"So, you think you are going to get away with community service, do you?"

"Sorry, sir; you tell me what to do".

"First things first, I want to talk to Little Sister. We will get her! But for the time-being maybe you can tell me if she helped you plan it".

"Plan it! Oh, no, sir, it just happened, it wasn't planned".

"Did she try to stop you?"

"No, she didn't realise I'd done it at the time. When she did, she gave me such a telling off. She said I wasn't civilised".

"So, why didn't she call the police?"

"Because she thought a telling off was enough".

The constable came in with the tuna sandwich and ice-cream. Placed the food in front of Gatwick, who finished it all off in no time.

"You say you're ready to sign a confession; is that right?"

"That's right, Inspector. When I've finished my fizzy drink".

"I see, when you finish your fizzy drink... In the meantime, can you tell me where your little sister is now?"

Gatwick nearly choked on his drink: "She's ... I can't tell you". He couldn't let Little Sister be arrested, such a sensitive creature, she would despair. Anyway, she was civilised. Then, there was Mama. If anyone found out that she was up on Emerald Mountain, they would shoot her. Gatwick didn't like telling lies, as an exception, just for this once, he had to.

"Because I don't know", Gatwick answered.

"When did you see her last?"

"Yesterday".

"Where were you?"

"Sorry, I don't remember".

"You had better get yourself a lawyer, you badly need one".

"What's one of those?", Gatwick asked.

"It's a person who will defend you. Who can speak for you".

"I don't need anyone to defend me. I can defend myself, and I can speak for myself" and, with that, Gatwick drank the last of his drink: "I've finished", he said.

"It's your choice. OK, that's it for today. You can sign the confession in the morning". The Inspector left.

What was Gatwick to do now? Looking around him, he thought that this wasn't quite like the Grand Hotel. There was a wooden bunk bed, a simple toilet, a small washbasin and a TV. He had better make the most of this. The top bunk seemed more exciting than the bottom one. So, Gatwick switched on the TV, climbed up the ladder, made himself comfortable and watched the news.

After a lot of talk about boring politics, which Gatwick didn't know anything about, they spoke about a big bank robbery that had taken place the day before yesterday. Someone was being questioned about it, the police thought they were on the right track. The police were continuing their search for others who might also have been involved. Though they assured the population that the super criminal they had behind bars was the brain behind the whole operation. They had an idea about where the money and gold bars were, but couldn't give information out about that just yet, so as not to prejudice the enquiries. The Chief Inspector appeared on the screen. Gatwick got excited because he knew the man. The Inspector made a statement: "We will get every single one of them. We have to send out a message to these criminals that dishonesty does not pay. We live in a civilised society and will not let criminals ruin what we have fought for for centuries".

"Mmmm, civilised?", thought Gatwick. That word came over his ear again. The police would do what was necessary to get these horrible criminals. He hoped they would get them soon because they certainly were not civilised.

He climbed down from the top bunk and thought he'd had enough now. It was time to go home. He tried the cell door, it was locked! Gatwick couldn't get out. He knocked on the door, but nobody came to his rescue. The only other way out was through the window above the bunk bed. That had iron bars running from side to side, and from top to bottom. What could he do? He'd have to stay the night. He switched the television off and put the light out, then he climbed onto the top bunk again and lay down, with his head on the pillow. Cuddling his wooden spoon, he looked up at the stars through the iron bars, until he fell asleep.

25 The Real Big Box on Wheels, Tied Up with Red Rope

That same evening big things were happening in the White Alp bunker: the Eagles were in a right kerfuffle. Stud was freaking out on the warpath. He had told Sam to go and fetch Jet and Bird Dog. He wanted them all there, to listen to what he had to say. All three birds were perched on the edge of their chairs, shivering with fright. The air in the bunker was as thick as glue. The smell of cow dung coming from

Gatwick's box was incredible, it clung and clung to everyone's nostrils. There were no windows to open and air the place. Then Stud started shouting at the three:

"How dare he put cow dung and garbage in the box! He must've known we were gonna take that there box, and he played a dirty trick on us. How did he know? I tell ya guys, no low-level trickster gets the better of me. Sam! Take that there box out, it smells like hell gone bad! Empty it, then store the box and the rope in the basement, ya never know when we might need them.

"You Bird Dog! Contact Miss Acid and ask her to go through CCTV footage carefully. I wanna know everythin' he did in the three days before he left London. I even wanna know how many times he went to the toilet: any suspicious movement! Anythin'! Go do that now and get outta my sight.

"Now, Jet! You dumbhead, did ya tell Gatwick ya were gonna take his box?"

"No, I never told him".

"Then, how the hell did he know?"

"No idea. Sorry, sir".

"That's great! That's so great, nobody knows. Who is this guy that he can run rings round me? Where is he now?"

"Sorry, sir, I don't know".

"Ya dunno! Jet you thick skull, now listen carefully to what I tell ya, I ain't gonna tell ya twice. Just go and find him and bring him here. Have ya got that? I've had enough of this, I wanna question the guy myself. It's the only way I can find out what he's up to. I can't rely on ya useless lot. D'ya hear me? Do me a service, willya? Get outta here pretty damn quick!!"

Jet left without knowing where to go. As he came out of the bunker he saw Sam trying to get the cow dung off his claws. It was spreading out in all directions because it had melted in the sun, and Sam was a bit slow.

"Now it's melted, I ain't got a clue how to get it away from the entrance here", he confided to Jet.

"Why don't you just leave it there, then", Jet suggested.

"Man, d'ya think I can do that?"

"Yeah, why not? Stud said to take it out of the bunker, and that's what you've just done, isn't it?"

"Man, ya so bang on. It ain't in the bunker, so it must be outta the bunker. Yeah, good thinking, I'm gonna leave it here".

Jet went off and thought he'd see if he could find a nest to sleep in that night. He'd go looking for Gatwick very early next morning, he'd be up with the larks. He would also get some worms then. Swiss ravens seemed to get up very early in the morning, long before English ravens, so Jet had to be quick off the mark.

26 The Imitation Big Box on Wheels, Tied Up with Red Rope

In the meantime, Dazbog had taken the imitation big box on wheels, tied up with red rope, to his superiors. Then Dazbog began to tell the General what he'd done:

"General, I tooked box from cub I meeted in Grand Hotel near Airport. He was with girl bear; she had suitcase full of money. I niever take suitcase with money because, you know, General, we don't need money. We've got so mich money from population, we don't know where to put more money: Ferrari, yacht, Grand Hotel, we got mich. I just taked box because I thinked would tell me you who they are".

"Comrade", the General answered. "I look, I look, just look now".

Dazbog started untying the red rope with his beak. Then he ran his beak along the sellotape, like you would with a pair of scissors. The box fell open.

"Vhat is this?" said Dazbog. "Paper, mich paper. Moment, moment, I read. Zis is all rubbich paper – crumbled little balls – I uncrumble them for you".

So he took out all the balls of paper from the box and unfolded them, ironed them with his claws and then placed them on a pile on the General's desk. They started reading the documents. Not that interesting. Invoices for office supplies, for bird seed, etc. Until after about fifteen minutes, Dazbog stumbled on a report, which read:

TOP SECRET MISSION

To: Regal Eagle, y'know where.

From: Stud, Bunker, White Alp.

Ref.   SBMB/REYKW

Date: 11/8/0011

PLAN TO BLOW UP THE KREMLIN

INTRODUCTION

The other day you asked us to investigate the possibility of blowing up the Kremlin.

FINDINGS

We can now advise as follows:

- it is a big place with many rooms;

- we suspect that they have burglar alarms;

- we spoke to the caretaker who advised that, despite the extensive security, it would not be that difficult to place bombs around Red Square;

- observation and discussion with other members of staff confirmed that this was true.

PRACTICES

Staff leave early to go home and drink vodka (which is cheaper than water, they are also given drink vouchers by the state for three one-litre bottles each per week).

COSTS

The cost for the operation will be 30% higher than expected: $ 50 million, though we have to allow for another increase in price. The increase does not appear to be justified. AW will provide the explosives. He will manufacture the bombs for us and detonate them when asked.

CONCLUSIONS

It seems the best time to blow up the Kremlin is in the evening when the staff are home and drunk. We do not want many casualties. The aim of the attack is to send a clear message – we need to make an impact.

I would like to recommend a meeting with you to discuss the gravity of the problem and to discuss possible improvement of performance.

THE END

The General of the Red Vultures and Dazbog looked at each other and couldn't believe their luck: the discovery of an attack at the heart of their government.

"You will be award biggest medal we have. We will even make new one especially for you. Dazbog I niever think you are best in our secret service. We need send more troops round Kremlin, keep eyes open for enemy want to put bomb. And, we also poison dis Gatwick".

27 The Morning After the Day Before

It was early morning and Gatwick was woken up by the clanging of a chain attached to the key of his prison cell. A security guard came in with his breakfast: honey puffs with full-fat milk and coffee.

"Do you have salmon", Gatwick asked, very nicely.

"No, I'm afraid we don't, sir. It seemed a bit off and we didn't want to give you belly ache".

"Oh, thank you. That's so nice of you. You know, at the Grand Hotel they gave us kippers as well".

"Well, our customer care service is probably not as good as theirs. Anyway, enough messing around now. Eat up because the Chief Inspector will be here in a moment".

Gatwick watched television while he had his breakfast. They weren't talking about criminals any more. There was a documentary about rooks. They were really horrible to each other, they called it 'war'. One big rook ordered some rooks to kill other rooks, even their own brothers and sisters. The TV cameras moved to another place. But there were more rooks there doing the same thing. There were images of rooks chopping other rooks in half using axes. Luckily,

Gatwick had finished his breakfast by then so wasn't put off his food.

The Chief Inspector walked in. "Here we are, Gatwick, we'd like you to sign this confession".

"OK, and then can I go?", asked Gatwick.

"No, you can't go whether you sign or not. It just makes life easier for me".

Gatwick wanted to please the Inspector and make life easier for him. Though, he'd locked the door of his cell, and wouldn't let him go, the Inspector did treat him quite nicely. But, they had a long way to go before they could come anywhere near to the standard of the Grand Hotel.

"Right, here we go. Sign here, on the dotted line?"

Gatwick drew a muffin on the dotted line. The Inspector didn't look at the signature. It had taken Gatwick about ten minutes to draw that muffin (because of the chocolate chips) and the Inspector had got fed up with waiting.

The Inspector told Gatwick that he was going to be questioned again and that the interview would be recorded:

"Anything you say may be taken as evidence and used against you", he told Gatwick. Now, let's talk seriously. Where's your accomplice, your little sister?"

"Sorry, Inspector I can't tell you that".

"OK, let's try another one. Where's the money?"

"The money? Why do you want to know that? It's mine".

"Oh, it's like that, is it?"

"Of course, it is. I was the one who had to scratch and scratch with my wooden spoon to get it".

"You mean to say that you got to the money using that wooden spoon!?"

"Yes, sir. That's right", said Gatwick proudly.

"And your sister didn't help you?"

"No, but she was there. She rejoiced with me and has helped me spend some of it".

"Where's the money now?"

"It's in her suitcase".

"Finally, we're getting somewhere. What does the suitcase look like".

"It's the latest model. It's a luxury Smartmite made of very tough ABS material. It's pink with silver trim and has two combination locks, which makes it the most secure suitcase ever made. When you open it, it plays *Knees Up Mother Brown*".

But, Gatwick didn't tell the Inspector that Mother Brown was his Mama. Otherwise he might tell the shepherds on Emerald Mountain, and they would shoot her.

"So where's the suitcase now?" the Inspector asked.

"Little Sister's got it. And, I can't tell you where she is, so I can't tell you where the suitcase is. So, please don't ask me again".

"I have news for you. We're going to look for your little sister and for that suitcase. You mark my words. We will get both, I promise you".

The Inspector left. Gatwick started watching television again. There was another documentary about rooks. It was in a different part of the world, but the events were the same. Rooks killing rooks. Baby rooks were starving to death, and they were dying of illnesses because they didn't have medicines. Some of the poor baby rooks were crying and some had flies all over them. Gatwick wished there was something he could do to help.

After the documentary, he thought he'd just lie in bed and look out of the window. He fell asleep proud of himself for not telling on Little Sister.

*

Jet had got up early, too. He went looking for worms and found some very juicy ones, indeed. The Swiss ravens were already around as well. When a worm was found, they stood in a line and voted on who was going to eat the worm. This they did by each raven putting its wing up when it wanted to vote. The Swiss called it 'direct democracy', and they were always doing it. They voted on everything. Jet was English so he just ate his own worms. He'd eaten so many worms that he had to rest a little before he could fly off.

He finally felt fit to fly. 'The best place to go', thought Jet 'is on Emerald Mountain, the last place I saw Gatwick'. So, up, up, up, he flew.

Little Sister and Mama had left the cave and were making their way up to the secret lake. Mama had to hide during the day. She didn't care for herself so much, but she knew Little Sister would be devastated if her Mama was shot and she was left all on her own. On their way up, they kept looking around to see if Gatwick was anywhere to be found. They kept shouting: "Gatwick, Gatwick, where are you?"

The two bears had decided to hide Little Sister's suitcase and Gatwick's Edwardian Case in the cave's secret extension that Bertie and Mama had carved out of the rock. They'd be safe there. But, they decided to take the fishing rod. They wanted to catch fish for lunch. Up the mountain they went, calling and crying for Gatwick.

Jet heard the shouts, then he saw the bears. Swooping down, he was soon in front of them.

"Hello, there. Little Sister, do you remember me? I'm Gatwick's best friend, Jet. We met at the Grand Hotel".

"Oh, yes", answered Little Sister. "We've lost Gatwick. We don't know where he's gone. He went out to play and never came back".

"Really? Do you think he's lost on the mountains?"

"We don't know where he could be. We don't even know if he's alive because he only had a waistcoat on and no food or drink. Such a pain in my heart. I was the one who sent him out", answered Mama.

Little Sister introduced Mama: "Jet, this is my mother and Gatwick's mother".

"Pleased to meet you", Jet said holding his wing out for her to shake.

She said: "Ciao", to him.

"Please, both of you, don't worry I'll look for him. I'll look everywhere for him. I've got to find him" Jet announced thinking of the punishment he'd get from the Eagles if he didn't take Gatwick to White Alp soon.

Little Sister and Mama Bear thanked him again and again. Jet flew off. The bears continued their climb up to their secret lake. When they got there, they took turns in fishing. In one hour, they caught ten fish. Far more than Gatwick had ever caught in one day!

Jet flew around over the mountains turning and twisting in flight, and spinning in the air. He could do all sorts of somersaults and make patterns high up in the sky. In the distance, he could see two helicopters coming his way. Who were the people in them, and where were they going? They kept circling round and round making such a terrible noise; disturbing the peace and the tourists. Jet saw some uniformed men in the helicopters, it looked as if they were members of the police force. Were they looking for Gatwick, too? Jet followed the helicopters. Maybe they would lead him to Gatwick. After circling the mountains a few more times, they turned around on themselves and started to fly away. Their destination was the police station. One of the police officers got out of the helicopter and went to speak to a man in plain clothes. Jet listened to their conversation:

"Sorry, sir, we weren't able to find her. We'll try again after lunch".

"OK, maybe she's hiding. Gatwick wouldn't tell us where she is. Such a stubborn bear. If he doesn't co-operate, he'll be in jail for the rest of his life".

Jet had understood it all now. Gatwick had been arrested for the bank robbery, Jet himself had seen it all from the rooftop opposite the bank. That would explain all the money he'd been splashing around. Well, who's crying now? Anyway, Jet had to get to Gatwick and take him to Stud. The Eagles would have Jet's guts for garters, if he went back without Gatwick. Jet flew all around the prison looking into every cell, until he found the one with Gatwick in it. The raven started pecking at the window to see if he could wake Gatwick up. Gatwick thought he could hear the pitter patter of rain on his window. 'It's so cosy to be in bed when the rain is beating against your window pane', Gatwick thought. It went on and on: pitter patter pitter patter... Gatwick opened his eyes to look at the rain and to his utter surprise, there, on the other side of the thick glass was Jet.

"Jet, Jet, my friend! Oh, Jet, you're always there for me".

"I'm going to try and get into the prison and help you escape. Do you hear?"

"Oh, yes, I do. It will have to be through the door. I can't get out through these prison bars. I've already tried, I'm too fat", said Gatwick.

"Don't worry! I'll find a way".

Gatwick was so happy. At last, he would be able to see his Mama and Little Sister again.

When a guard went into the prison, to start his afternoon shift, Jet flew in through the door; swiftly and stealthily so nobody would notice him. Then he flew around to look for the right cell. 'I think it's this one', he said to himself. He picked at the lock with his beak. It wasn't easy-peasy. Not at all. He had to turn it so that it would unlock, but they used such heavy locks in prisons. He tried again, it moved a little way round. Gatwick was standing on the other side of the door anxiously with his wooden spoon in his paw. On the right track. Let's try again. This time, the lock moved further, one last wrench. Yes! It's done. The lock went round one full turn. Now, the door was unlocked, but Jet couldn't push it open. It was too heavy.

"Can you pull it from that side, Gatwick, it's unlocked?" Jet asked.

Gatwick tried to grip the door handle, but it was too high. The wooden spoon came to the rescue. Gatwick held it up as straight as he could, placed it on the inside of the handle and pulled and pulled until the door opened. There was Jet, on the floor exhausted, he panted:

"You see, Gatwick, I told you I'd get you out!"

"Oh, Jet, Jet, my best friend. Thank you so much for freeing me. You are my saviour!"

"Well, I wouldn't put it quite like that".

"Yes, you are, you are. How can I ever thank you?"

"Let's get out of the prison first, it's not going to be easy", whispered Jet. "People don't usually take much notice of birds. If they see me, they'll just try and chase me out with a broom. But, bears, that's a different story. Especially, here in Switzerland. You know, they shoot them".

"Yes, I know, but only when they're big".

"That's true. By the way, I met your Mama up on Emerald Mountain. They'll be after her".

"You met my Mama? And, did you see Little Sister, too?"

"Yes, I did. They were leaving their cave when I saw them this morning. Very worried about you, they were. I told them not to despair, that I would look for you".

"Oh, Jet. I can't wait to see them again. It wasn't too bad in here, but they locked the door and I couldn't get out".

"Course, they lock the doors, it's a prison not Disneyland".

Gatwick didn't know what he meant. As long as he could see his family again, he didn't care about understanding, or not understanding, things.

"Gatwick, we need a disguise to get you out".

Gatwick had left his sunglasses and fake sideburns in his Edwardian case, or were they in Little Sister's lime-green leather handbag? Whichever, they weren't here.

"There's nothing in this room that I can wear". Gatwick poked his head around the door. He saw a bin, he could put that over his head.

"Wicked!", exclaimed Jet. "You'll look like a lampshade. You won't see where you're going, but I will direct you and tell you to stop when someone's coming".

After closing the door carefully, with the help of his wooden spoon, Gatwick ran to the bin, turned it upside down, crawled under it, and stood up.

"Walk straight on, five more paces then turn left, go on, straight ahead, now go down ten steps". Jet could see a prison officer approaching. "Stop!" Gatwick stopped in his tracks. As he passed Gatwick, the prison officer thought it was strange to have a lamp right there at the bottom of the stairs, and one with furry legs, too! Very strange. This young man had only been working at the prison for two days, perhaps he'd never noticed the lamp before, maybe it was new. He tried to think what the reason was for furry legs holding up a lampshade. He couldn't think of anything.

When the prison officer climbed to the top of the stairs and turned the corner, Jet instructed Gatwick to start walking again. Straight on again, now stop because we've reached the prison entrance. The door was locked and bolted. Difficult.

"I know", whispered Gatwick. "Fly around the place and flap your wings as hard as you can. When they notice you, they'll get a broom, and try to hit you out. They've got to open the door to do that".

"Great idea!" said Jet.

So Jet starting flying around the prison, flapping his wings hard and making a loud whirring noise. The prison warden soon noticed Jet, he'd never seen such a big black raven before. 'What's a raven doing in here?', he thought. 'How did it get in?' He went to get an enormous broom and, right enough, he opened the heavy steel door of the prison entrance, waved the broom about, and hit Jet out. Gatwick went from standing dead still just inside the prison doors, to standing dead still just outside the prison doors. 'Another lamp with furry legs' the prison warden, thought to himself 'are these all the go nowadays?' He didn't follow fashion much.

As soon as the door was closed shut, Gatwick threw the bin off himself and started running as fast as his furry legs would take him. Jet swooped down and said:

"Steady, Gatwick, first we've got to pay a visit to a friend of mine. He wants to talk to you. Really, don't worry about it because he can be very nice, when he wants to".

"Jet, any friend of yours is a friend of mine. But I do so want to see my Mama and Little Sister".

"No, we've got to go and see my friend first. Look, if it wasn't for me you'd still be in prison. Please just do me this favour and then you can go back to your family".

Gatwick thought he had better keep Jet happy. After all, he was such a great friend.

"Oh, come on, then; let's go to your friend".

Jet took the scruff of Gatwick's waistcoat in his beak and flew him to White Alp and Stud. It started raining hard, Gatwick and Jet got soaking wet. The White Alp cave was soon in sight. But, there was such a horrible stink. Can you imagine Gatwick being transported through the air in Jet's beak with a wooden spoon in one paw and holding his nose with the other?

"I thought mountain air was supposed to be pure and clean", Gatwick shouted up to Jet.

"Yes, well there was a consignment of cow dung, and it ended up at the entrance of the Eagles' cave. First, it melted in the sun and now, I suppose it's getting mixed up with rain water. At least it will be washed away".

Gatwick just squeezed his nose as much as possible, the smell got worse and worse. He knew they had reached the cave because the smell was unbearable. Jet flew Gatwick in and consigned him to Sam.

"Hi man. Did ya have a good flight?", without waiting for Gatwick to answer, he pushed him into a cell saying: "Ya stay in here till ya called for", and then locked the door. Gatwick didn't like locked doors. He wanted to be able to walk in and out of a room as he pleased. There was just a chair and a television in the cell – no bunk bed – maybe he wasn't staying the night. He thought that he might as well watch television to pass the time away. They were talking about other birds now: sparrows. They showed images of them dying in droves, whole areas were flooded and they were drowning. Some sparrows were selling little female sparrows as slaves to bigger birds and even to men. Gatwick really couldn't understand the world of birds, nor that of people either.

It seemed to Gatwick that the answer to the world's problems was in one word: love. There didn't seem to be much of that around. If only they were all like bears and felt what Gatwick felt for his Little Sister, Mama and his friend Jet. What a silly lot birds and people were.

28 Miss Acid's Emails

In the meantime, Stud was reading two emails from Miss Acid. The first email was about Little Sister. Miss Acid had enquired with the airline. Her findings were that Gatwick had an accomplice on the flight; a female who could be described as all white with red ears, a cherry-red, heart-shaped nose, red soles on her paws, and a red dickie-bow round her neck. A member of the crew had given Miss Acid a plan Gatwick had drawn of the plane. There was a drawing of the bear in the seat the little white bear had sat in. This surely was extremely compromising. His accomplice had flown on the same flight.

The next set of enquiries regarding the little white bear were carried out in Lugano City Airport. Security staff there had checked CCTV footage for Miss Acid. It was clear that the little white bear had jumped into Gatwick's box. If they had nothing to hide, why was she travelling in that box?

"What a woman! That Miss Acid is really somethin'!" Stud exclaimed, "If only all the spies we Eagles have around the world were as clever as she is".

He had to put her in for promotion. Maybe JFK Airport in New York, surely she was wasted at Gatwick Airport.

The next email from Miss Acid was even more interesting. She herself had been through all the CCTV footage of the few days before Gatwick left Gatwick Airport. As clear as anything she'd seen in her life, there was Gatwick speaking to Arnold White, the big polar bear. They talked for a very long time indeed. It was also very clear that Arnold White had given Gatwick something. A close-up showed that it was some kind of silver coin, maybe a token of some sort.

Stud couldn't believe this. He summoned Bird Dog and Sam telling them to be pretty sharp about it.

"OK, ya two now just perch ya fat backsides on those them chairs a moment. What I'm gonna tellya is gonna shockya. I know that anyone can be anyone, I've been in the spy trade for years, but this is the most surprising case yet".

"Hey, sir, so what's your problem?" Bird Dog asked.

"Shut it a moment willya? I'm gettin' there ya jerk. It's like this: Gatwick has been captured on CCTV at Gatwick Airport talkin' to Arnold White for a long time. Arnold's body language suggested destruction. And, before he left, Arnold gave Gatwick a token. Probably to open up lockers at Gatwick Airport. D'ya two fat heads know what this means? Ya don't get it, d'ya?"

Bird Dog and Sam looked at each other. Well, yes, in actual fact, no, they didn't get it.

"It means that Gatwick is in the pay of Arnold White. It means that Gatwick is Arnold's spy. It means that Gatwick through Arnold White has always been at our service".

Now for readers who have never heard of Arnold White here is a quick run up. Arnold White, also known as Anton Weiss, is without doubt the most powerful creature on our planet. In other words, he can make mincemeat of the world, shove it into sausage skins and send it out into space. Under the guise of selling ice, he is the biggest arms trafficker in the world. In the North Pole, he has warehouses full of all sorts of arms and ammunition, anything you could think of: from hand guns, to rockets, to missiles, and to atomic and nuclear bombs. Up in the North Pole, Eagle Knevil, Arnold's chemist genius, toys with red mercury and plutonium every day. Arnold only needs to press a button to trigger a nuclear reaction. He knows how to handle detonators and he can overthrow any government. In short, the world is in Arnold's hands.

"You don't say!?" exclaimed Bird Dog.

"It's a helluva problem we got here, sir; I just threw Gatwick in one of our prison cells".

"Then you go get him out, ya thick skull. Bring him here, we gotta make it up with Gatwick before we upset Arnold".

29 Little Sister

Back in Lugano City prison, the Chief Inspector was making his way to Gatwick's prison cell. He was going to question him again, especially about the whereabouts of his sister and the money. The heavy metal door wasn't locked. "Strange", he thought. He put his head round the door, and his suspicions were confirmed: Gatwick had escaped! The inspector scratched his head and wondered how Gatwick could have done that. Only a highly sophisticated brain could plan such an escape in such a short time and carry it out. And, Gatwick didn't seem that intelligent – but he must have been very, very clever to pull this off. Wow! That had never happened before. The Inspector rushed to set the alarm bells ringing. All the staff ran to search the prison itself and some then got into jeeps and drove all around the surrounding fields. Gatwick was nowhere to be found.

"Send the helicopters out again. I want that bear and his sister here now!" the Inspector shouted.

The police were also soon out in full force and whizzed their way to Emerald Mountain. He had to be up there.

Little Sister and Mama were on their way back from their hideout. Up near the lake, they had found an injured sparrow. Mama had cut one of her apron strings off with her teeth and had bandaged the sparrow's leg. She placed the little bird in her apron pocket and decided to take it back to the cave, so she could nurse it until it was better. When they arrived back in their cave, they started making lasagne... but, then they heard a noise at the cave entrance. Little Sister ran to the entrance thinking Gatwick might be back. Mama ran after her.

"Hello, can I come in, please?" It was Jet.

"Oh, Jet. Yes, of course, come in. Have you any news about Gatwick?", Mama asked.

"Yes, he was arrested by the Swiss Police. I found out he was in prison and I helped him to escape".

"So, where is he now?", Little Sister asked.

"He's with some friends of mine. But when he's finished talking to them, I'm sure they'll bring him here".

Oh, the relief to know that he was still alive and well.

"Do you think he'll be back this evening in time for my lasagne?" asked Mama.

"I don't know about that. I wouldn't bank on it", Jet replied.

"Well, you can join us, then?"

"No, I'm so sorry I've got to be getting back. I just wanted to let you know Gatwick's OK".

"I'll come with you a little way until you take flight. Thanks so much for bringing us news of Gatwick", Little Sister insisted that she should accompany Jet.

"OK", Mama agreed, "but don't dilly-dally on the way, you know how worried I get".

So, Jet and Little Sister set off. One thing Jet hadn't realised was that the Swiss Police were following him. They had recognised him when they flew past him in their helicopter. Jet had showed up on the CCTV footage in the bank robbery scene, he was perched on the rooftop opposite the bank. Probably, another accomplice.

Jet flew off. One of the helicopters followed him. They couldn't catch him; he twisted, turned and span. The helicopter was not as agile as Jet. The other helicopter crunched its way to Little Sister. She ran as fast as her little furry legs could go. Then, she stopped to think: if she ran back to the cave, the police would find Mama in there, it would be leaked out that there was another adult brown bear on Emerald Mountain, and she would surely be shot. Little Sister gave herself up to the Police. If Gatwick had been through this, she could endure it, too. And, who knows, Jet might come and help her escape. She stood there, quite still, waiting for them to land. A man came towards her, and showed her his identity badge. Following him into the helicopter, she thought of Mama, how devastated she'd be to be on her own, without her little cubs. Poor Mama! But, at least she was safe, nobody would shoot her.

They locked Little Sister in a cell similar to the one Gatwick had been in but in the female wing of the prison. Soon the Inspector arrived.

"Now, little Miss, I just want to ask you a few questions about last Friday" began the Inspector. "Do you remember where you were?"

"Oh, yes. That was the day we went shopping. We bought a handbag, a suitcase and some chocolates. Oh, and we also went to the bank".

"What did you go to the bank for?"

"To get some money. We got lots and lots, then we put it all in my suitcase".

"So it was a big amount. Do you know how much?

"No, sorry, all I know is that half was in francs and the other half in pounds".

"How do you know that?"

"Well, Gatwick asked me how I wanted the money".

"So, you knew about this?"

"Well, of course, that's what we went to the bank for".

"Don't you think that Gatwick did something very wrong, very uncivilised?"

No! Now she realised why she was there. Gatwick had dropped litter. She remembered how she had started crying because he was not civilised; how Gatwick had felt so guilty. "Inspector, I am so sorry for what my brother did. I think that being civilised means that you always do the right things. Doing the wrong things means that you will go to jail".

Now Little Sister was worried. She continued:

"I promise you that he will never ever do it again. I will make sure of that. I hope you will forgive him. We didn't think anyone saw us. Really, he'll never do it again".

Then Little Sister burst out crying: "I told him he shouldn't do it, and I did tell him off".

"Well, it's too late for that now. You're an accomplice. Will you sign a confession?"

"Yes, of course Inspector. I'm very civilised, though I don't know what 'accomplice' means. I might be that as well".

"Where's the money now?", asked the Inspector.

Little Sister wasn't going to do something as stupid as to tell him that. Not because of the money, but because the suitcase was in the cave with Mama and, if they found the suitcase, they would find her Mama:

"I'm so sorry, Inspector, I can't tell you that".

"Why, can't you tell me?"

"Because I don't know".

"I don't believe you. We're going to look for that suitcase. You mark my words. We will get it, I promise you, whether you tell me where it is, or whether you don't".

"All right, Inspector, I'll tell you the truth. I know where it is, but I'm not telling you!"

"OK, we'll talk about that later. For the time-being, we'll get your confession drawn up. I'll be back soon. Do you want anything to eat or drink?"

"Yes, please. Could I have a fizzy drink and some chips?"

"Fine, I'll see what I can do. By the way, that necklace you're wearing. Where did you get it from?"

"Oh, this? It was a gift from Gatwick. He found it".

The Inspector went off thinking what a strange pair these two bears were. He was quite confused, couldn't believe how easy it had been to get them to confess. But, they really did not want to hand that money back. He called a prison warden and told her this cell had to be guarded 24 hours a day. One escape was enough. What would public opinion be of the police now?

*

Mama Bear cried in despair. All she had left to keep her company was that little lame sparrow. She cried and cried. "Mannaggia! Damn it!", she wailed. "God, I have such a pain here in my heart. First I lost my Bertie, then I lost my son, and now I've lost my daughter. Why?! Why?!" She threw the lasagne out of the cave entrance and it rolled down, down all the way into the valley below.

30 Stud and Gatwick

Gatwick was still watching television in his cell in White Alp. He'd been watching some well-preened brainless robins, cavorting around, flaunting their legs and their breasts. He thought he was a show-off, but these were just something else. He'd soon got fed up with those and started watching some owls on another channel. The show was called Universal Challenge. Four owls were sitting in a row, above another four who were sitting below. A rooster was firing questions at them telling them to: "Come on!" That was the same rooster as he'd seen talking about the warring rooks. Universal Challenge was too difficult for Gatwick, so he switched it off. As he was looking around him, to see how to keep himself busy, his cell door opened. It was Sam:

"Oh, Mr. Gatwick. Our boss Mr. Stud, would like to invite ya to his office".

"Fine, I'll be up in a moment. Could you carry my wooden spoon up for me, please?"

"Of course, sir. This way", Sam beckoned to Gatwick, unfolding his wing to show him the direction.

"Nice red carpet you've got here, a very fluffy pile, very soft to the paws".

"Yes, sir. I'm glad ya find it to ya liking".

Gatwick entered the room. Stud and Bird Dog stood up. They held out their wings and gave Gatwick's paw a hearty shaking.

"Would ya like to sit down?"

Gatwick said: "Thank you", as he took a seat.

"How was your trip here?" Stud asked.

"Pleasant, I've always liked travelling. But, that smell at the entrance here. Well, it's really bad".

Stud didn't know what he was talking about so let that pass: "Can we offer ya a drink and some food, sir?"

"Oh, yes, please I'd love a fizzy drink, a tuna sandwich and some ice-cream".

"No, problem. Sam, could ya go get Mr Gatwick what he asked for".

"Yes, sir!", and off Sam went.

"Mr. Gatwick, ya might be wonderin' why we called ya up here. I hope ya didn't take it bad. We simply wanted to meet ya and tell ya how much we admire ya. Also, we wanted to give ya a gift to show we're friends of yours".

Sam came in with the fizzy drink and food. Stud had to wait for Gatwick to finish eating and drinking before he could continue speaking.

"As I was saying there, I want ya to accept a token of our appreciation. Sam, can ya go and get the box from the basement".

Sam went off again, while Bird Dog kept smiling at Gatwick. There was an awkward silence so Gatwick started indulging in small talk:

"Rotten weather, isn't it?"

"Oh, ya, ya, really rotten. I haven't been out in a long time. Really, rotten, eh, Bird Dog?".

"Oh, ya, ya, really, really rotten", agreed Bird Dog.

"The sun keeps coming out and going back in, it doesn't know what it wants to do, does it?" Gatwick said.

"No, it doesn't know what to do, it keeps coming out", agreed Stud.

"No, it doesn't know what to do, it keeps going back in", followed Bird Dog.

Thankfully, Sam came back with the box.

"Hey, that's my box. I had it stolen from me!"

"Believe me, Mr. Gatwick. We found it, and we brought it back here for safekeepin'. Ya know we didn't want it to get lost".

Gatwick didn't ask any questions, he had got his big box on wheels, tied up with red rope, back and that's all that mattered. Well, what a surprise, never in a million years would he have expected to see his box again. And, right here of all places!

"Well, thank you so much, thank you".

"Walk this way, Mr. Gatwick, and we will fill it up for you".

Gatwick trundled his box along behind him to the store room, even the wheel had been fixed properly!

When the door to the store room opened, Gatwick saw so much money in there that he thought it was fake.

"Is it real?" he asked.

"Of course it's real. This is the reserve of the federal bank, I tell ya".

"Well, thank you very much for showing me your money. Can I go now?"

"Just a moment. Sam here is going to fill your box up. Would you like pounds, francs or dollars?"

"Mmmm. Can I have some of each, please?"

"Of course. Sam fill the box will ya?"

"Yes, sir. Of course, sir", replied Sam.

"Goodbye, Mr. Gatwick and if ya need anythin' in the future, just give us a call. Or, come up and see us, now you know where we are".

"I certainly will", Gatwick assured him, "any friend of Jet's is a friend of mine. Oh, and by the way, thank you for the fizzy drink, sandwich and ice-cream".

After the box had been filled to the brim, and the red rope tied up nice and tight, Jet was called to accompany Gatwick to wherever he wanted to go. As far as the Eagles were concerned, they'd managed to avoid the world coming to an end for the foreseeable future.

He was the happiest bear alive, off to see his Little Sister and his Mama. At the entrance of the cave, Jet took Gatwick by the scruff of his waistcoat again. Gatwick held his wooden spoon in one hand and the box in the other: "Take me to Emerald Mountain, Jet!"

They arrived after about an hour's flight. Mama was so pleased to see Gatwick that she started crying: "Bambino mio, bambino mio, bello!" She hugged him, she kissed him, and hugged him again. "Saint Lucia has answered my prayers".

"Where's Little Sister?" asked Gatwick.

"Bambina mia, bambina mia, bella!" she repeated, "they've taken her away in a helicopter, Jet told me".

"Yes", Jet agreed, "Little Sister had been taken away by the Swiss Police. I watched it from a distance, they tried to get me, too. But, I managed to escape. It was strange but she didn't put up a fight, she didn't run back to the cave to take refuge".

"She did it to protect me, mia bambina bella", sobbed Mama.

Gatwick explained to Jet:

"If the Swiss shepherds find out that Mama is here on Emerald Mountain, they'll shoot her like they shot my father, Bertie. They believe that she would kill their sheep, but she wouldn't because she doesn't eat mutton or lamb. Let's sit down and think about what to do". Gatwick started to think and put his finger on his chin. "We've got to work out a plan, we've got to get Little Sister out of jail".

"It's not as simple as you think, Gatwick", argued Jet. "After your escape they will have stepped up security. I can't get her out, the way I got you out. They'll have a guard on her door 24 hours a day".

"So, there's only one way, isn't there? We've got to talk to Stud. He said if I needed help he would be ready to give me a hand. Let's go and see what he can do for us. I'll take my Edwardian case, with my sunglasses and fake sideburns, with me just in case I need to disguise myself". He put his wooden spoon in the case as well, and off they went.

Mama cried. She didn't know if they were tears of sadness or joy. Her family might all be together again soon. The thought made her so happy. She wanted to celebrate by making some spaghetti with goat's cheese, followed by fillet of fish, and apple crumble and custard for dessert. She took the sparrow out of her apron pocket, and placed it on a little feather bed she had made for it. 'Now, let's get down to work', she said to herself putting her apron on.

*

Stud was very surprised to see Gatwick back so soon. What could he want? More money? Was he going to dry up the federal reserve? Stud thought he'd better call up Bird Dog as witness. This time, Jet was at the discussion, too. Gatwick began:

"Mr. Stud, I know you my friend, as I said before any friend of Jet's is a friend of mine. Although, I wanted to go home rather than come here after being released from prison by Jet, I want you to know how glad I was to meet you. You offered me kind hospitality by providing me with a fizzy drink, tuna sandwich and ice-cream, gave me my beloved box back, and filled my box with money. Now I want to ask you to do me a huge favour on the strength of our friendship".

"Well, ya know, Gatwick, I will do anythin' in my power to help ya. D'ya need more money?" Stud felt cornered. You can't say no to someone who is the spy of the most powerful being in the world. Stud had no choice; he had to do whatever Gatwick wanted. 'Let's just hope he doesn't ask the impossible', Stud thought to himself. These were the people who were going to blow up the Kremlin for the Eagles.

"Oh, no, please, I don't want any more money. I have so much I don't know where to put it. No, what I need is for you to help me get my Little Sister out of prison. She has been wrongly accused of being my accomplice in a crime I committed last Friday. She is totally innocent".

"I'll do what I can. We can do it in two ways. We can either talk to the Prison Director and Chief Inspector, or we can blow the place up", Stud said confidently.

"I think you'd better talk to them. Little Sister would be so frightened if she heard explosions, and we don't want to frighten Little Sister, do we?"

"Hey, ya dead right, no way do we wanna frighten your little sister. That's a deal. I'll phone 'em and scare the hell fire outta 'em".

"Thank you so much. I'm sure I can return the favour in future".

Now, that was like music in Stud's ears. Someone as powerful as Gatwick saying he will be on their side in the future –

excellent – they needed to keep their dominant position in the world and force freedom on every stubborn nation which didn't agree with them.

"Mr. Gatwick and Jet, do you mind, going downstairs to our sitting-room, while I make a few phone calls?"

"No, of course, not", replied Gatwick.

Gatwick and Jet left the room, then Stud picked up his big red phone:

"Hello, there, can I speak to the Director of the prison, please? This is White Alp Eagle speaking".

"Hold on a moment, Mr. White Alp Eagle, I'll put you straight through on our priority phone line".

The telephonist knew who White Alp Eagle was.

"Ah, good day to you Stud, how can I help you?" said the Director.

"Good Day to ya, Walter, how are ya? Look y'know I try to disturb ya as little as possible, don't ya?"

"Yes, I haven't heard from you for a long time".

"Well, I need a big favour from ya. Ya have a little white bear in that there prison of yours, she goes under the name of Little Sister. I think she's been arrested for bein' an accomplice to a crime committed by Gatwick".

"Oh, yes, they pulled off one of the biggest bank robberies of all time. Then we arrested him, and he managed to escape – we still don't know how he did it or where he is".

"I ain't surprised. D'you know who he is?"

"I've already understood that he puts on an innocent appearance, but that he's really very shrewd".

"He's only Arnold White's spy. Do y'know what that means?"

"My God, I had no idea. That explains it, do you know that he signed his confession by drawing an explosion of an atomic bomb – yes, like Hiroshima".

"There ya are then, what did I tell ya. Ya gotta let her go".

"Yes, yes, you're right. But, what do I do about public opinion?"

"Sorry, Walter, that's your problem. I got enough of my own problems up here. I'm sure ya'll work it out".

"Fine, Stud, leave it to me. Can you send someone round to fetch her? Or, do you want me to accompany her".

"Give her something to eat. Her brother and Jet, a raven, will come and meet her. I'll sent Sam, too. Jet can only carry one of the bears in his beak".

"Fine, I'll do what you asked. By the way, Stud, thanks for telling me all this. We could have been in big trouble, if we'd carried on with these proceedings. Bye for now".

"Bye and thanks a lot".

The Prison Director phoned the Chief Inspector and told him about the telephone conversation.

"You've got to lay off this little bear, I'm sorry", the Director told the Chief Inspector.

31 The Bank Robbery

The Chief Inspector was devastated – all that work. He'd given up his weekend, worked nights even, to follow through this investigation. All for nothing. What was the use of pouring all that effort into work if this is the outcome? Nothing! It was no use. He would have to start all over again. "Luigi, go and get me that CCTV footage, let's go over it again". The Inspector sat there patiently going through the footage again with his assistant. It was clear to them that the bears were guilty. But, the police had to feed public opinion with culprits otherwise they would think the police were incompetent.

"The only thing we can do", suggested Luigi to the Chief Inspector, "is to put the blame on those workers. Yes, I know it's not fair, but they were the only other ones around. They're like us, you know, Inspector, they work and work for very little satisfaction".

"Yes, I agree with you, Luigi; sometimes we have to do unpleasant things like that. Have them arrested and bring them here".

The Inspector made his way to Little Sister's cell. When he got there, he told the guard to go home, there was no need for him any more. The prisoner was being released, she was 'not guilty'.

"You mean to say, I've been standing here all this time for nothing!", the guard said.

"Afraid so. She's being released".

"They just brought her another bowl of chips, sir. I think she'll want to finish those first".

The Inspector went in. "Hello, Miss Little Sister, I'm glad to see you are enjoying your stay".

"Oh, yes, very much thank you, sir. Please let me finish my chips, and please also don't ask me where the money is. I can't tell you".

"No, Miss Little Sister. You can keep your money. Mr. Gatwick should be arriving any moment now to pick you up. We're letting you go".

"Oh, Gatwick, my big brother. I can't wait to see him again!"

"Yes, we'll go to the main entrance and wait there".

"It was about time you let me out. I was starting to get bored here. Not much to do. How do you stand it?"

The Inspector didn't answer that one. He was so fed up with these bears, glad to see the back of them. They waited at the entrance for a few minutes, until they saw a cub and two birds coming their way in the sky. They got closer and closer, and were dipping ready for landing. The bears were so pleased to see each other after all that time, they kept hugging and kissing, hugging and kissing. Then, Sam said:

"Come on, ya guys, stop freakin'. We've gotta get outta here".

So Jet took Little Sister by the back of her red dickie bow, and Sam hooked Gatwick by his waistcoat. Off they flew to the cave in Emerald Mountain.

32 The Cave

Mama's joy was immense when she saw her little ones again. She was so overcome with emotion. "Oh, my bambini, you are both safe. The pain in my heart was so strong. Saint Lucia answered my prayers. Thank you Jet, and thank you Mr. Eagle for bringing my babies back to me. Now, let's be happy. Let's celebrate. Let's eat!"

Mama brought out the spaghetti in an enormous terracotta bowl. There was enough to feed an army.

"Come on, eat up, eat up; and be happy", she kept repeating.

Jet and Sam had never tasted worms as delicious as these.

"Hey, Mama, ya got the recipe for these here worms", asked Sam, "I'd sure like to cook these for Stud".

"My dear, I always make my recipes up as I go along, anyway they are top secret".

Sam could relate to that. Secrecy is of the essence. He asked if he could have a little more please.

"Of course, eat up, I like my guests to have a healthy appetite".

After he had finished yet another bowl of spaghetti, he thought it was time to get going.

"You want to go already!", exclaimed Mama. "But, we've only just started eating. You've got to try the fillet of fish.

"Oh, my God!", pleaded Sam. "I can't eat any more".

"Yes, you can", argued Mama. "I'm sure you've got a little space in the corner of your stomach for Mama's best fillet of fish. What is it? Don't you like my cooking?"

"I love your cooking, it's just that..."

"Then come and eat, and be happy".

So, Sam had two big helpings of fish, followed by two slices of apple crumble and custard. After that, he explained he really had to be going – his country needed him.

After bidding Sam 'goodbye' and thanking him over and over for his help, the bears settled down to doing the dishes. When all the washing up was finished, Gatwick went to get a box of chocolates for them to share. Jet was invited to eat chocolates with them and stay; he accepted.

That evening, the bears and Jet discussed their future. They all came to the conclusion that living in the cave in Emerald Mountain was too dangerous for Mama. Also, going up to the secret lake every day was fine while she could still manage it. There would come a day when she'd be too old for that climb. No, they had to find another solution. They had to go back to Gatwick Airport. Now, the only problem would be to get Mama down the mountain without being seen. To go down the mountain in the daytime was impossible; they would spot her. They couldn't go on foot at night because it was pitch black, they'd get lost. Impossible. Jet said he couldn't fly her down because she was too heavy, his beak would break. The only way was for her to disguise herself and go down by train with the others.

They decided they would leave early next morning and catch the first train down. There were always fewer people around at day break. Gatwick would walk in front of Mama, and Little Sister behind her. Jet would fly around the area and make sure there were no hunters. If there were, he would peck them in the face.

That night they started getting their belongings together.

155

Mama wanted to take her dinner set because it was a wedding present from Bertie's parents; and she had a lot of memories of the good dinners she'd had on those plates with Bertie. They packed the pieces of the dinner set, layering them with the money so that they wouldn't get broken. It was sad for Mama to leave the house she'd shared with Bertie, but she knew he would have wanted her to be safe. He would not want her to be in danger and, anyway, she was now starting a new life with her little ones who brought her so much joy.

So early in the morning, they all got up and started putting their plan into action. First, Mama unwound the bandage from the little sparrow's leg. She perched it on her paw: "Tweet, tweet", she chirped to it, kissed its head, then told it to: "Take care of yourself, now fly high, you're a sparrow". Off the sparrow flew, it span around once to wave 'goodbye' to the bear family. They had been so kind.

Now Mama had to disguise herself. Gatwick gave her his sunglasses and fake sideburns. She had better wear her apron too, they decided. Little Sister took her red dickie-bow off and placed it around her Mama's neck. "We think you should pull my suitcase", said Little Sister, "so you look like a tourist".

They started towards the train station. The journey was along the narrow rocky footpath, jutting out of the mountain. A sheer drop was to their left, there were no barriers. On the other side of the deep valley were other similar mountains. As they made their way down, they had to keep an eye on the mountains opposite for shepherds with binoculars and rifles. They came to a particularly dangerous elbow bend sloping downhill rapidly. Little Sister held on to Mama's apron string. "Tread carefully here, my dears", she warned the two little bears, "one footstep out of line here would lead to tragedy". A strong wind seem to conjure up from nowhere. It raised the dust which blew into their eyes making it difficult for them to see where they were treading. "Slowly, here, my cubs, slowly", warned Mama. "We'll be there soon". They got around this blind corner, the footpath became easier. Here they walked a little more briskly.

But, coming around that bend meant that they had come into the sight of a shepherd. He had been lying in wait. Through his binoculars, he looked across the valley. The creature in the middle looked very much like a brown bear to him. His rifle was loaded, he placed it into position and took aim. His finger pulled the trigger. At the same time, Jet flew in his face and pecked his nose as hard as he could, this made the shepherd's arms rise, and the shot was fired into thin air. The man had fallen backwards, Jet sat on his face, jumped up and down while flapping his wings. What a terrified shepherd he was. Jet's intervention gave the bears time to go around another bend, and out of the shepherd's view. In the distance, the bears could now see the train station. Their impulse told them to run, but caution made them continue their steady pace.

They were approaching the station when the train arrived. Jet was there, too; he saw them onto the train and flew down to the flatland and to the railway station in the valley. After forty minutes the bears arrived, safe and sound. They were relieved and happy to see Jet again.

"Now", Gatwick began, "let's get a taxi to the Grand Hotel. I think we could spend a couple of nights there and then go back home".

Everyone agreed with him, especially Little Sister who remembered how she'd been pampered there: "Exciting!", she shouted: "Why don't you come with us in the taxi, too?", Little Sister asked Jet.

"I'd much rather fly, thank you. See you there", and off he flew.

The bears opened and ate another box of chocolates to celebrate the escape.

33 Five-star Life Again

Now feeling quite at home at the Grand Hotel. Gatwick confidently walked up to the reception desk.

"What rooms will I give you?", the receptionist asked, surprised to see Gatwick and Little Sister in the hotel again, and this time with their mother and Jet.

"I'm sorry to remind you", began Little Sister, "but we never got our sweets last time".

"I gave you one suite", answered the receptionist, "I distinctly remember it".

Now was not the time for arguing.

"Could we have four sweets, please?", asked Little Sister.

"I'm so sorry, but I only have two left".

"Fine, we'll take those two", declared Gatwick.

"Yes, Mama and Little Sister take one, and you two can take the other", said the receptionist pointing to Jet and Gatwick.

"Could we have a marshmallow and a Turkish Delight, please?"

"I see", the receptionist smiled. Only now had he understood that they meant 'sweets'. "Of course", he nodded, "and would you like some toffee, fudge, and perhaps a lolly or two?"

"Yes, please", they all sang out together.

Gatwick and Little Sister decided they would show Mama and Jet around the hotel: the swimming pool, whirlpool, sauna, and Turkish baths. They would try them all out. Mama was most impressed by the whirlpool. She'd never been in one before, all those bubbles tickling you. What luxury!

And so it was that their second stay at the hotel started out in the best of ways, if it hadn't been for the Red Vultures in the suite between their two suites.

In the last few days, the Red Vultures had also been out looking for Gatwick and Little Sister; but others had seemed to get to them first. Now, though, the Red Vultures had had the good luck to have the bears come and stay right next door to them. The Red Vultures weren't sure if Gatwick was a friend or an enemy of theirs. It could work out in three ways:

First, Gatwick might have been carrying the documents for someone else, and didn't know anything about the mission to blow up the Kremlin; this option seemed unlikely to the Red Vultures.

Second, Gatwick might be working for Anton Weiss in which case he was their friend. Because Anton Weiss was their man. He pretended to work for the Eagles, under the name of Arnold White. But, if anything was going to be blown up by that powerful polar bear, then it would be done when the Red Vultures gave him the OK.

Third, Gatwick was working for the Eagles and had no idea Anton Weiss was spying on the Eagles for the Red Vultures (and making pretend that he would blow up the Kremlin). Gatwick might believe that the attack on the Kremlin was really going to happen.

In the first case, they would simply let Gatwick go off scot free.

In the second case, the Red Vultures would have to treat him like a prince, a powerful friend.

In the third case, the Red Vultures would feed Gatwick a powerful nerve poison. This would cause him nausea, vomiting, diarrhoea and stomach cramps after about three hours. Then after about another three hours he would die the most painful slow death.

Dazbog started going around the hotel in the hope of meeting one of the creatures in Gatwick's party. He couldn't see any of them. Quite understandably, the three bears were sleeping after all the stress of the escape. But, Dazbog spotted Jet in the gardens looking for seeds.

"Mpnbet", Dazbog said 'Hello' to Jet.

"Mpnbet", Jet replied, it must have meant 'hello' he thought.

Dazbog thought this a good start. If he understood Russian, he must have been one of them. Jet didn't like to be disturbed while he was looking for seeds. Jet thought he'd just answer 'no' to all his questions. If he didn't show interest that might get rid of that big bully of a bird. Just as you think you've got some peace and quiet for yourself, someone has to come along and spoil it. So, Jet decided to answer his questions by saying 'no':

Хороший день не это?

"No", answered Jet.

Вы остаетесь здесь длинными?

"No".

Я люблю это, здесь не делают Вас?

"No".

Jet's technique of answering 'no' didn't seem to be working. Maybe he should try answering 'yes', instead.

Вы с ребенком Тэдди?

"Yes".

Вы работаете с ним?

"Yes".

Вы знаете Антона Веисса?

"Yes".

Вы в его обслуживании через ребенка Тэдди?

"Yes".

Вы ...?

Jet had lost his patience. In good wholesome English, he squawked viciously:

"Beat it, willya?"

Here is the translation of the dialogue between Dazbog and Jet. Those of you who do know Russian can go on to the next chapter.

"Nice day, isn't it?"

"No", answered Jet.

"Are you staying here long?"

"No".

"I love it here, don't you?"

"No".

Jet's technique of answering 'no' didn't seem to be working. Maybe he should trying answering 'yes', instead.

"Are you with Gatwick?"

"Yes".

"Do you work with him?"

"Yes".

"Do you know Anton Weiss?"

"Yes".

"Are you at his service through Gatwick?"

"Yes".

"Are you ...?"

As quickly as he could, Dazbog moved away. He had got a glimpse of Jet's nasty side and didn't like it.

34 Trouble for Little Sister

Wandering around the hotel, a little later on, Dazbog found Little Sister in the swimming pool whizzing down the long slide shouting: "Wheeee!" with a strawberry lollipop in her paw, a beautiful diamond necklace around her neck, and the hotel's plastic shower cap on her head. While Mama was having her afternoon nap, Little Sister had quietly crept out of the suite and made her own way down to the pool.

Dazbog dived into the pool at the point at which Little Sister would fly off the slide and bumped into her on purpose pretending he was there by accident:

"Very sorry, Miss little white bear", he apologised.

"Don't worry about it, I'm having so much fun!"

"Haven't I seened you here before?"

"I don't think so, I don't remember you", she answered.

"You in room next to mine".

"I've never noticed you before. Would you like to whizz down the slide with me?"

"I'd love to whizzed. Let's go!"

They climbed the steps to the top. Little Sister sat down ready for the dive: Dazbog snuggled up behind her. As they were about to slide down, Mama appeared at the door: "What's happening here?" she yelled across the swimming pool. "Get away from my little girl, you greasy vulture. How dare you?"

Dazbog got up, flew down the steps and then out of an open window.

"I'd like a word with you, Miss", Mama said sternly to Little Sister. "Go up to our room straight away. The moment my back is turned you go off and get yourself into trouble".

Once in their room, Little Sister sat on her water bed quite abashed. She still had her lollipop in her paw, the hotel's shower cap on her head and the diamond necklace on.

"I've told you many times not to speak to strangers, especially to male strangers".

"Yes, Mama: but he was so nice, and great fun".

"You are not old enough to judge who is good and who is bad. Do you remember the story of Little Red Riding Hood? She thought the big bad wolf was good. But, he wasn't, was he?"

"No, Mama: he was bad, very bad!"

"There you are then. Now as punishment, you won't watch TV this evening and you will go to bed without dinner".

"Yes, Mama".

So Little Sister looked for something interesting to do. Suddenly, she jumped to her feet, dashed to the dark wardrobe, went inside and looked up. There she saw a heavy metal box whose door was open. She couldn't reach it to see what was inside. She went into the bathroom and dragged the stool into the wardrobe. Standing on the stool, she gripped the edge of the lower part of the safe and heaved herself up. It was dark in there. Very dark, but she could see there was something in the left-hand corner. She looked again. Yes, there was definitely something there. What could it be? She heaved herself up some more until she managed to raise her leg up enough for it to enter the safe. Wobbling and wriggling around a bit, and pulling her other leg up behind her, she caught her diamond necklace on the lock on the inside of the safe door. And, as she entered the safe with her whole body, the door clamped shut.

There she sat in the dark and hadn't got the slightest idea what to do – she started crying. "Well, it's no good crying", she said to herself. Putting her paw down, she felt a hard cold object. It was what she had been trying to look at. But she couldn't see it now! It felt like a stone. Yes it must be a stone. Somebody must have brought it up from the garden and placed it there. With the stone, she started hammering on the safe door in the hope that Mama would hear the noise. Nobody came. Little Sister cried some more. The necklace was cutting into the back of her neck. She felt around for the clasp, and unfastened the necklace for relief. Then, she kept hitting the door harder with the stone, her heart was thumping and she was still sobbing a little.

Mama was having a bath. She was fully immersed in all that scented bubble bath froth. She was happy whistling then began singing:

"Don't worry, be happy

Oooooh, oooooooooh, oooooooh

Somebody came and took your bed

Don't worry, be happy

Oooooh, oooooooooh, oooooooh"

"That's enough soaking for the afternoon – time to be dressing for dinner.

Oooooh, ooooooooh, oooooooh,

Don't worry, be happy".

She dried herself all over with the hairdryer. "I once wrote a catchy poem about happiness and washing yourself", she said to herself. "How did it start? Oh, yes:

There's nothing like a piece of soap

To chase the blues and stop you mope

From when I was just six and a half

Every night I've had a bath

When I am soaped all over

I think of foamy waves in Dover

After I've sat amongst the bubbles

I forget my cares and muddles

I am happy as can be

When all those suds wash over me"

She thought that was a really good poem. One day she'd write a book of poems.

"Oooooh, ooooooooh, oooooooh,

Don't worry, be happy..." Mama sang, as she swayed to and fro dancing.

Then Mama Bear sat down on the... where was the stool? She was sure there had been one there. She'd have to go and look for it. But, first she wanted to fill the kettle and have a nice cup of tea. She briefly thought of the happy days she'd had with Bertie. There was a long pause in her thoughts, then she set off hunting around for the stool. "How could it have got inside the wardrobe? Silly place to..." Thump, thump, she heard, from the safe. There it was again, thump, thump. She gave it a tug, the door flew open and Little Sister rolled out still grasping the stone in her paw. Mama slammed the safe shut, turned the dial, then looked at Little Sister. "I'm afraid I don't quite understand why you were in there!"

"Please don't shout so loudly, Mama. I noticed that the safe was open and wanted to look inside, I got tangled up in my necklace and I locked myself in".

"Do you think that was a sensible thing to do?" asked Mama.

"No, Mama, I'm sorry. I knocked and pushed and kicked the door for a long time. I was so frightened..."

"Well, you're out now, don't think of it any more, my pet".

"Yes, Mama. You know, my necklace is still in the safe". She thought that having a dickie bow around her neck was really quite enough decoration. That heavy shiny thing only weighed her down. "It didn't look nice with my dickie bow, Mama. Let's just leave it in the safe", Little Sister suggested. "I'd rather have the stone. The necklace got me locked in, and the stone got me out".

"Whatever makes you happy, my little one", Mama said affectionately.

35 The Hero

In the meantime, in the other suite, Gatwick was waking up after his afternoon nap. He got up to look for Jet. Where was he? Because he was in a five-star hotel, Gatwick thought he had better smarten himself up a little – brush his fur properly – something he hadn't done much lately. So, he carefully groomed his head, tummy, legs and paws. The fur on the top of his head had started growing again, he noticed. At the back his fur was still ruffled. He couldn't reach there, so left it. Have you ever seen a bear who is neat and tidy at the front and scruffy at the back?

In the enormous, well-lit reception hall, Gatwick and Dazbog's paths crossed near the fountain.

"Excuse me", began Dazbog holding his wing up signalling Gatwick to stop. "Can you tell me way to swimming pool?"

"Oh, yes, you have to go down two floors, the pool is on the right at the bottom of the stairs".

"Thank you so mich. Eh... Are you in suite next to mine?"

"Yes, I believe I am", replied Gatwick.

"Yes, you were here before few days ago. Have you beened here on business?"

"I'm not sure that's any business of yours", Gatwick answered, a little irritated at his direct manner.

"I so sorry, not very civilised of me to ask".

"That's true, it's not civilised", said Gatwick. Then he thought that he hadn't always been civilised either. He ought to forgive Dazbog:

"No, problem. Don't worry about it. Let's go and have a drink together", Gatwick suggested.

So off they went to the hotel bar for fizzy drinks.

"I speaked to your friend, Jet, in garden this morning", started Dazbog.

"Jet's my very best friend, you know. He's helped me to escape twice. Once when I was hiding in a plastic bag at Gatwick Airport, and the other time from prison".

"So, you beened in prison?"

"I have, but I don't want to talk about it, if you don't mind".

"So, you travel lot?"

"Well, I do my fair share", answered Gatwick, trying not to show off too much.

"I beened in prison, too, you know", admitted Dazbog.

"Really?"

"Yes, when I did something for big white polar bear. Have you ever meeted big white polar bear?"

"Yes, I have. At Gatwick Airport".

"Have you ever meeted big white polar bear in pin-striped suit?"

"Yes, I have. He gave me some money. I know all about his activities".

"Can you remember what company he work for?"

"North Pole Iced Solutions".

"That's right!"

"Yes, his name is Arnold White, but I know he also calls himself 'Anton Weiss'".

"Arnold White? You say he has two different names?"

"I don't see anything wrong with that. For example, my father had two identities, he was a vicious killer to some, and was loveable to others. He was known as Gilbert Brown to some, as the Brown Bear to others, and simply as Bertie to his family".

It suddenly dawned on Dazbog that Gatwick's situation was

much more complex than had seemed. Not only was he a great spy, but his father had been one too. Gatwick had been in prison, for shady reasons, while his father had been a killer. Dangerous, a very dangerous family. Not only. Anton Weiss was obviously working for the Eagles under another name: he was double dealing, selling arms and ammunition to both the Eagles and the Vultures. Now, how could anyone know which side he was really on? Would he blow up the Kremlin? Probably, because he just wanted to sell as many bombs as he could.

Dazbog flew up to his room, phoned the General at their Headquarters, on their hotline, and informed him about his findings. "You never going to believe this...", he began, "but I just founded out most incredible information. Anton Weiss double-dealing us..." and so Dazbog told the General the whole story.

Then, Dazbog exclaimed: "Gatwick was only one who knowed this. He knowed very mich. And, we niever knowed this terrible truth till now. Gatwick on our side or he wouldn't tell me information".

After the General had listened, with utmost interest, he decided that the only way out of the situation was to give Gatwick a big reward in money, for two reasons. The first, for telling them this vital secret information and, the second, to keep him quiet. Of course, someone as astute as Gatwick would understand. "Give him back his big box on wheels, tieded with red rope, and fill with mich money. If you not enough money there, I send you mich money".

The next day, early in the morning, the courier arrived with packets and packets of money. Dazbog packed the imitation big box on wheels and tied it up with red rope. As soon as he'd finished, he went to Gatwick's suite and rang the bell. Jet was already out looking for worms. Gatwick was still dreaming about chocolate. He thought he heard the bell, but didn't know if it was in his dreams or for real. That happened to him every now and then. Sometimes, when he was thirsty at night, he dreamt that he was drinking water, and it really quenched his thirst. Strange!

Anyway, after he'd tried opening the door in his dreams, the bell still kept ringing. So, he had to get up to answer it. Well, of course, Gatwick was especially mega-ruffled first thing in the morning. He stumbled to the door, and found Dazbog standing behind it.

"Hello, there. How come you're up and about, at this time of day?" asked Gatwick.

"It 10.30, you know".

"Exactly, how come you're already up?"

"I bringed you your big box on wheels, tieded with red rope. You know, I finded it".

"Thanks, so much, Dazbog. Just put it down there, please. I'm still a bit dazed, I think I'm seeing double. Are those two boxes right there?"

"Yes, two box there. Well, I go now. Comrade want to see me. Bye, and good flight home".

Dazbog left and Gatwick went straight back to bed. And, dreamt some more about chocolate. He slept until he had slept out all the sleep in him.

Mama and Little Sister had already packed. And were ready to leave. Where was Gatwick? They went to his suite and rang the bell again and again: 'ding, dong, ding dong, ding, ding'.

"Come on, Gatwick, let's go", Little Sister shouted behind the door.

Gatwick opened the door and let them in. He showed them the two identical big boxes on wheels, both tied up with red rope. He asked them if he was seeing double. "No", they assured him, "there are two". That's what Dazbog had said, too. So, without any idea why this was so, they set off for the airport, each trundling a piece of luggage. Before they checked their luggage in, they sat on a bench in departures and took the two remaining boxes of chocolates out. They ate one box between them and put the other box back saving it for their flight home.

Handing luggage over to airlines can be risky. Suitcases do not always end up where they should. Gatwick hadn't realised that all the suitcases he'd climbed up at North Terminal had been lost by someone – some passengers never saw their suitcases again. Especially those whose suitcases had finished at the bottom of the pile or in the middle.

When they arrived at Gatwick Airport, they waited and waited for their luggage, but... it didn't appear on the conveyor belt. Maybe the bears had gone to the wrong baggage reclaim! No, they couldn't see their luggage anywhere. So all three of them went to the Lost Luggage Desk.

The lady behind the counter looked at her computer. "We're very sorry", the lady apologised, "we don't know where your luggage is. Let me just make a phone call. Excuse me, please..."

She spoke on the phone for quite a while.

"Look, we're so sorry, your cases seem to have gone to Lisbon. The baggage handlers thought the cases were going to Lisbon and not London, they misread the destination. I'm sure they'll arrive tomorrow", she reassured them.

"Don't worry about it, we can come back tomorrow, we live here", Gatwick replied.

They were glad to be home. Gatwick was so proud of his home. He led Mama and Little Sister to his broom cupboard. And that's where they slept that night – under the mops.

36 Eat and Be Happy

In the morning, Gatwick showed Mama and Little Sister around Gatwick Airport. First, they went to look for left-over muffins and half finished cups of coffee. Gatwick had looked everywhere for his muffin map, but he couldn't find it: 'someone must have thrown it away', he thought. Then, he took them to the pizza hut. But, it was empty; it had closed down. Where would they go for food? They were going to find it hard to get enough to eat in future.

Then, Gatwick wanted to show his family the airport entrance, and the area outside, where the buses stopped. Gatwick told them which buses went where. He also showed them the bus shelter where he had slept, and got his fur drenched, that night when Miss Acid had thrown him out. And, all of a sudden Jet came flying by.

"Hi Jet; when did you get back?" Gatwick asked.

"Late last night", he answered. "Did you know that Miss Acid has left? She's now head of security at JFK Airport in New York".

"Yippee!" That was one change that Gatwick welcomed very much indeed. No longer would he have to spend sleepless nights on a cold and wet bench. Gatwick told Jet about the closure of the pizza hut. Jet was shocked, he used to get a good crust or two from there. What now?

"Do you think we should move to another airport?" asked Jet.

"No", replied Gatwick, "this is my home".

"Let's go and look at the notice in the restaurant window, let's see if it's going to open again. Maybe they're on holiday", said Jet.

"I don't think so, it was completely empty", Mama Bear pointed out.

"Let's go anyway", Little Sister said.

So, off they went to the empty restaurant. The notice read:

RESTAURANT TO RENT

DEAL ALSO INCLUDES 4 ROOMS AND 2 BATHROOMS

ALL NEWLY-REFURBISHED

EXCELLENT OPPORTUNITY

Then followed all the contact details, which they didn't bother reading.

"What does 'rent' mean?", Gatwick asked.

Mama and Little Sister revealed that they'd never ever been there, so they didn't know where rent was either. Jet knew what it meant. Some of his friends had rented a chest of drawers to nest in, somewhere on the outskirts of London.

"What you do", Jet explained, "is to give someone money to let you use something they own". Now that he had explained it, it sounded complicated to him: "You can have the restaurant for as long as you give them money every month". The bears understood now.

"Let's go and see if our luggage has arrived. I'm a little worried about my dinner set", said Mama.

So, they all headed for baggage reclaim. The lady saw them coming and recognised them at once.

"Oh", she said, "I was just thinking of you. Your luggage is here". And, there they all were piled up against the wall. Little Sister was so chuffed to see her pink suitcase again that she danced a light jig. They trundled their luggage to the broom cupboard.

"Why don't we rent the restaurant?", Mama said.

Gatwick thought they ought to sit down and think. He placed his finger on his chin and asked Little Sister what she thought: "I think it's the greatest idea ever".

"OK, let's phone them". They all went to look at the number on the notice, then wandered off to the nearest phone box.

"Hello!" Gatwick said."I'd like to rent the restaurant at Gatwick Airport. Have I got the right number?"

"You certainly have", answered the agent.

They decided that the viewing would take place that afternoon. The agent told them that if they signed the contract and paid the first three months' rent in advance, they could have it straightaway. The bears loved the idea. When Mama saw the kitchen, she couldn't believe her eyes – she didn't know that such well-equipped kitchens existed. She put her apron on there and then. The living quarter round the back was spacious and had big windows. Seeing their enthusiasm, the agent whipped out the contract and showed Gatwick where the dotted line was. Gatwick drew a muffin on it, paid the man and the deal was done. A quick hand-paw shake, and Gatwick was given the keys.

The agent gave them the phone number of interior designers for restaurants, and for the living quarters, John Lewis had everything they needed. Gatwick phoned them as soon as he could find the right coins. They didn't waste time in coming round and measuring the place up. Soon the whole lot was newly-furnished – it looked as good as the Grand Hotel they'd stayed at.

The bears invited Jet to live with them, but he said he preferred the outdoor life. He would come and give them a helping wing during the busy periods. Flying is very handy, if you're a waiter. Of course, Jet would have all the free food and drinks he wanted.

The bears took down the notice from the shop window and replaced it with a new one:

COME IN !

GREAT MENU ONLY £10

For that you get:

spaghetti

ice-cream

fizzy drink

*

LOOK AT ALL THE SPAGHETTI WE'VE GOT:

spaghetti with hamburgers

spaghetti with fat chips

spaghetti with smoky bacon

spaghetti with fish fingers

spaghetti with salt and vinegar

spaghetti with steak pie

spaghetti with crinkled chips

spaghetti with sausages

spaghetti with tuna sandwich

spaghetti with potato wedges

spaghetti with baked beans

spaghetti with curly wurlies

spaghetti with chicken nuggets

spaghetti with cheeseburger

spaghetti with thin chips

spaghetti with crisps

spaghetti with yorkshire pudding

spaghetti with shepherd's pie

spaghetti with egg and bacon

*

AND LOOK AT ALL THE DELICIOUS ICE-CREAM WE'VE
GOT:

Italian ice-cream made by Mama: 50 different flavours

*

FIZZY DRINKS

Any colour you like

*

MUFFINS

A free chocolate muffin for every customer

*

With Mama as cook and the little bears and Jet as waiters, the place became an enormous success. People from miles around came to eat at the restaurant, even if they weren't catching planes. Passengers started flying from Gatwick Airport rather than Heathrow, and to make sure they got a table the smart ones booked their table over the internet soon after they'd booked their flight. Some passengers missed their planes, for second helpings. Eagles, vultures, ravens, hawks, rooks, roosters, sparrows, and other birds the bears didn't recognise, all went to eat delicious worms there. It was a place where you could dine with celebrities and where spaghetti was free for the homeless.

After closing time, the bears got down on their paws and furry knees and cleaned and polished the whole restaurant until it was spick and span. Their hard work and friendly service resulted in their getting: The Best Restaurant of the Year Award.

Every hour, on the hour, Mama would come out of the kitchen and join Gatwick and Little Sister in the aisles, between the tables, where they danced to the tune of *Knees Up Mother Brown* for two minutes and a half. Even Jet took part when he was there.

For the dancing, Gatwick wore his red waistcoat and his red Christmas tie. Some of the more outgoing customers joined in dancing with the bears. The name of this awesome restaurant was:

THE END

Send Gatwick Bear an email and tell him what you think of his story!

gatwickbear@rocketmail.com

About Book Binding

Sewn

Before the 19th Century books were bound by sewing the pages together by hand. Around 1850, automation began with the advent of functional sewing machines. The process of stitching pages became much faster. Soon after, David McConnell Smyth designed the first sewing machine specifically for binding books. A small quantity of sheets (usually eight) are folded down the middle to form a section (usually of sixteen pages). These sections are known in the book trade as 'signatures'. Signatures are sewn together along the folds. This method of sewing is still known as "Smyth Sewing". The latter is the best way to bind books because books can lie flat when open and their pages will not fall out no matter how many times they are read. Most Sparkling Books are Smyth Sewn.

Wire or Spiral

A few Sparkling Books will be wirebound, especially plays. This is to allow directors and actors to turn the pages at 360 degrees while rehearsing.

Glues

Most pages of the books you buy are now glued together. This process of binding books was introduced at around the time as paperback covers in the 1930s. The positive aspects of glued paperbacks were that the prices of books dropped dramatically and books became accessible to a wider population. On the other hand, quality was sacrificed.

There are different methods of gluing:

Cold Glue Binding

Over time, cold-glued bindings become brittle which causes pages to fall out. Glued books will not lie flat when opened and the pages tend to fall out if this action is forced. And, when one page falls out, the rest tend to follow.

Hot Glue Binding

Books bound using hot glue will last longer than cold-glued bound books. However, with time, they too will come apart. Nowadays many hardbacks are glued to keep costs down.

The Thermoplastic Strip

Thermal adhesive strips are similar to glue binding and have the same limitations.

Sparkling Books

David Kauders, *The Greatest Crash*

Carlo Goldoni, *The True Friend / Il vero amico*

Gustave Le Bon, *Psychology of Crowds*

Alexander Pushkin, *Marie: A Story of Russian Love*

Ilya Tolstoy, *Reminiscences of Tolstoy*

M.G. Lewis, *The Bravo of Venice*

Grace Aguilar, *The Vale of Cedars*

Harriet Adams, *Dawn*

For more information visit:

www.sparklingbooks.com

Sparkling Books